MAELSTROM
Ilsa Mayr

You can't go home again, popular wisdom claims, but Merrilee Ingram, singer on hiatus from a concert tour, ignores the warning and returns to her Appalachian hometown. Almost immediately, the campaign to run her out of town begins and quickly escalates from verbal threats to snake drawings to a live Copperhead on her porch. Someone in town has a memory long enough to remember that, as a child, Merrilee was deathly afraid of snakes.

Meeting the town's boss and society maven, Merrilee is shocked by the hatred the woman and her daughter display toward her. They, too, ask her to leave. Police Chief Quentin Garner wonders if the threats are rooted in the suspicious death of Merrilee's mother, which a four-year-old Merrilee witnessed. Will she remember what happened before the murderer can strike again?

Other books by Ilsa Mayr:

The *Cybil Quindt Mystery* series:

Alibi for a Cold Winter's Night
Banker's Alibi
A Timely Alibi

Serenade
Summer Flames
Portrait of Eliza
Gift of Fortune
Dance of Life

MAELSTROM

•

Ilsa Mayr

AVALON BOOKS
NEW YORK

Published by Thomas Bouregy & Co., Inc.
160 Madison Avenue, New York, NY 10016

Library of Congress Cataloging-in-Publication Data

Mayr, Ilsa.
    Maelstrom / Ilsa Mayr.
        p. cm.
    ISBN 978-0-8034-9968-3
    I. Title.

    PS3613.A97M34 2009
    813'.6—dc22
                    2009003539

PRINTED IN THE UNITED STATES OF AMERICA
ON ACID-FREE PAPER
BY HADDON CRAFTSMEN, BLOOMSBURG, PENNSYLVANIA

To my husband

Prologue

"**R**un!"

Still half-asleep, the little girl whimpered as her mother lowered her to the ground through the open window of the cabin. The flames cast an eerie light over the familiar place.

"Run and hide in our magic place in the woods. Do you hear me?"

"Yes, Mama. But it's almost dark."

"Don't you dare cry. And since when are you afraid of 'almost dark'? I'll come for you as soon as I can. After he's gone."

The woman looked at the child hard, willing her to obey. "Run," she said again, "before he sees you."

Not understanding the reason but hearing the desperation and urgency in her mother's voice, the child turned toward the woods. She ran until she reached the tall trees. There she stopped to look back at the cabin.

The flames were now shooting through the roof. The girl whimpered again.

Suddenly she saw the figure of a man outlined against the fire's light. She heard him call her name. Caught between her fear of the dark woods and of the man, she instinctively chose the woods.

Eerie and dark, the forest closed around her. The branches tried to grab her, the uneven path to trip her, the darkness to trick her sense of direction. Driven by measureless fear and the ever closer voice of the man, she ran until the big rock blocked her way.

Remembering all the times she'd come here to play, she dropped to the ground. The entrance to the magic place had to be here. She crawled until the thrashing sounds of the man running through the underbrush froze her into immobility.

Curled into a tight ball, a fist pressed against her mouth to stop the whimpers, she waited in mindless, animal terror.

Chapter One

"That girl's back. Reba's redheaded sin child."

Pet's coffee cup clattered into her saucer, spilling the heavily sugared black liquid over her mother's second-best breakfast cloth. "Here in Browne's Station?"

"No, over to Louisville." Lurlene shot her daughter a sarcastic look before she picked up the crystal bell beside her plate and swung it vigorously several times.

As soon as the tinkling stopped, Pet asked, "Why did she come back? Does she know what happened?"

Lurlene shrugged her plump shoulders. "For her sake I hope she doesn't."

"But why would she come back here?"

"Her mother's buried here. To some children that means something." Lurlene glanced meaningfully at her daughter. "Besides, this is her hometown."

"It isn't as if she was treated real nice when she lived here." Pet picked up the pack of cigarettes she'd brought

3

with her and tried to shake one loose. Several fell onto the tablecloth. Her crimson-nailed fingers trembled slightly when she placed a filter tip between her lips. She flicked the initialed silver lighter several times without success.

"Do you have to smoke at the breakfast table?"

Pet jerked the cigarette out of her mouth and tossed it next to the pack. "I'm upset, Mama. You know why."

"Take one of your nerve pills." Lurlene tore a biscuit in half and heaped it high with raspberry jam.

"Aren't you worried, Mama?"

Lurlene's bejeweled hand jerked slightly, causing a blob of jam to fall onto her shelflike bosom. She dabbed at it with her napkin. When she stopped, it looked as if fresh blood had soaked her white satin robe.

"What are you going to do? No, don't tell me." Pet pressed her napkin against her mouth. A slight shiver raced down her bony back.

Lurlene's voice contained a trace of contempt when she said, "That's right. The less you know, the better off you are." She stuffed the biscuit into her small rosebud mouth. She chewed greedily and lustily.

Pet fumbled with the catch of her pillbox. Aware of her mother's black eyes watching, a small sound, half-exasperated, half-terrified, escaped her throat. Finally she managed to push a pill between her lips and wash it down with water.

"Stop that pitiful mewling," Lurlene ordered in a low voice. "You know Odessa's probably got an ear pressed against the door this very moment."

As if on cue, the door opened.

"I swear, you're moving slower than molasses in January," Lurlene snapped at the uniformed maid. "Fetch a clean cup for Miss Petulia and a fresh dish of grits. These got cold."

"Yes, Miz Lurlene." Odessa picked up the unwanted dishes. She left the room as slowly and deliberately as she had entered it.

In the kitchen, she set the dishes on the counter. Turning to the cook, she said, "Miz Lurlene wants fresh grits."

Della looked up from the copper-bottomed pot she was drying and nodded.

Almost as an afterthought, Odessa asked, "Who's the girl that got back to town? Reba's daughter? The one the ladies in there are scared of?"

Della dropped the pot. Her hands flew to her mouth. "Miss Lurlene said Reba's girl is back?"

"Sure did. Miz Pet done took a nerve pill, and it ain't even ten o'clock yet."

Della whipped off the smock she wore over her yellow and white striped cotton shirtwaist dress. "Odessa, you got to do me a favor. Fix them grits. I gotta go see Otis real quick."

High on Laurel Mountain, where the two-lane blacktop widened into a tourist lookout spot, a top-of-the-line Lincoln waited, its powerful motor purring smoothly. The driver tossed a half-smoked cigarette onto the gravel, where a number of other butts smoldered. He glanced at his watch. Then his eyes focused again on the road where it disappeared behind the outcropping of granite.

Absentmindedly, he tapped his fingers against the steering wheel in time to the music floating from the radio. When he recognized the vocalist, he muttered, "Bitch," and hit the off button with his fist. In the sudden silence he heard the expected car before it rounded the bend.

The official vehicle drew alongside the Lincoln until the drivers' windows were aligned.

"Where have you been? I've been waiting forever."

"Sorry. A little official business kept me. What's the matter? You look as nervous and touchy as a sore-tailed cat."

"I'm not nervous," the man in the Lincoln lied. "But you have to admit, it's mighty queer her coming back like this. Especially now."

"Maybe she just got homesick for the old place in Browne's Station. Maybe she wants to show off her Mercedes, or maybe she wants to visit her aunt." The sheriff shrugged his shoulders.

"And maybe she remembered something about that night."

"After all these years? Naw. Besides, what could she remember? She was only four, and it was dark. Relax."

"That's easy for you to say. You don't have as much to lose as me," the man in the Lincoln said.

"I don't have as much money, but I got plenty to lose."

"Don't you forget that."

"Are you threatening me?" the sheriff asked, his voice hard.

"No, no. I'm making arrangements to have her watched. We'll know every move she makes. If it looks like she's on to something, well, how hard is it to get rid of one songbird?"

"Let's not do anything rash," the sheriff warned. "Remember, I'm not the one who acted rashly twenty-five years ago. Don't forget that." He touched two fingers to his hat in a parody of a salute and drove off.

"I may have to do something about you," the Lincoln's driver muttered. A murderous expression settled onto his face.

Otis sat on his front porch, whittling a piece of wood. He didn't pause when Della brought the pickup to a screeching stop mere inches from the porch railing.

Jumping out of the truck, she called, "Guess who's back?"

"I'm sure you'll tell me. How come you left the Buford place in the middle of the morning?"

"To tell you the news." Pausing beside his rocking chair to catch her breath, she demanded, "Otis, are you listening?"

Keeping his eyes on his whittling, he said, "I always listen to you, sugar pie."

"Reba's ditch-edge girl is back." A grimly satisfied smile flitted across Della's thin face. "I thought that might make you stop your infernal whittling."

"Hoo, boy!" Otis scratched his white-whiskered chin with the back of the blade. "Who said she was back?"

"Miss Lurlene. Odessa overheard her. What are we going to do?"

"Do? Not a blessed thing."

"Otis, we can't not do nothing."

"Stop whining. We haven't done nothing wrong."

"We didn't tell what we saw all those years ago. That was wrong."

Otis's arm shot up, and he clamped his hand hard around Della's bony wrist. "Listen to me. We didn't actually see anything twenty-five years ago. We only put two and two together and hinted to certain parties what we suspected. It got me an early medical disability from the mine and you a job with the old tub of lard."

"Don't call Miss Lurlene that. If she ever heard you, she'd fire me for sure."

"No, she wouldn't. Greedy Gut is way too fond of your cooking. Now go back and stop worrying."

"But, Otis—"

"Hush up." He stopped her protest by squeezing her wrist again until she winced. "I'll handle it. Haven't I always?"

"Yes, Otis."

"Now go back to work." He had a couple of aces up his sleeve to protect himself. Yes, sir, he wasn't worried at all. Whistling softly, he set the sharp blade against the wood.

"I followed the instructions in your letters to a tee. Do you have any questions?" the attorney asked.

Merrilee Ingram looked up from the document she'd been reading. "Everything looks okay. I now own Miss Willadean's house free and clear, right?"

"Right." Sam Stewart studied the elegantly dressed young woman sitting across the bare desk from him. "Miss Ingram, will you satisfy an old man's curiosity by answering a few questions?"

Merrilee nodded.

"Why the secrecy? Why buy the house under the name of a corporation? Who's Reblee, Inc., anyway?"

"I'm Reblee, Inc. I hired a very good and very expensive investment consultant who advised me to incorporate for tax purposes. The secrecy?" Merrilee paused for a moment, composing her reply. "Even though I'm not exactly a household name, I do have a following. Fans can be persistent and intrusive. I value my privacy."

The attorney smiled his thin-lipped grin. "Will you answer another question?"

"Probably."

"Why did you come back to Browne's Station?"

"Why not? It'll take months for my lead guitarist to recover from his latest car accident. I'll use the time to write some new material for the group. For that I need a quiet place to work."

"There are hundreds of quiet places in Kentucky alone, not to mention the rest of the country. So, why here?"

Though Sam had asked the question in an offhand manner, Merrilee caught the serious undertone in his voice. "Mr. Stewart, what, exactly, are you trying to find out?"

"You come straight to the point. I like that."

"And what is the point?" she asked.

Sam lifted his narrow shoulders in an elaborate shrug. "I find it difficult to understand why someone like you would return to a backwater place like this."

"I told you. I need a quiet place. Granted, there are lots of other towns I could have chosen, but I'm familiar with this one. Besides, here people will ignore me. You know what they say about prophets in their own country."

He smiled, but Merrilee realized he was still unconvinced. "Are you suspecting me of coming back to show off how well the little orphan has done for herself?"

"No, of course not," he assured her.

"Well, I might have, if I were a superstar. But I'm only moderately successful."

"You're too modest. Even I have heard your songs, and I don't follow the popular music scene. One more question and I'll shut my mouth. Why did you pick me to handle the purchase of the house? I can't even begin to describe myself as moderately successful."

"Now *you're* too modest. I remember Miss Willadean's saying that despite your . . . uh . . . unfortunate love of the bottle, you had integrity."

He smiled faintly, ruefully. "Your aunt never minced words."

"Miss Willadean wasn't my aunt. She provided a foster home for me because she took one look at my unruly red hair and decided I needed the firm hand of a churchgoing woman—and also because she needed the money. Those were her exact words. She never claimed any lofty or sentimental reasons for taking me in. As you said, she was brutally frank." Merrilee stood up. "Thank you for your help, Mr. Stewart."

He rose too, buttoning his seersucker suit jacket, which hung loosely on his tall frame. Bowing slightly, he said, "If I can be of further assistance, Miss Ingram, please let me know." He handed her his calling card. "My home phone's on the back. Feel free to call me at any time about anything. I mean that."

"Thank you."

On the way down the steep flight of stairs, Merrilee replayed the attorney's words in her head. Had there been a cautionary note in his voice, as if he expected her to need his professional help again? What would make him think she'd need help? With a shake of her head, she dismissed the tiny warning bell from her mind.

Merrilee drove the few blocks to the house on Oak Street with a mixture of eager anticipation and dread. When Willadean had died unexpectedly, her will had surprised everyone. Though she had taken the precaution to disabuse her ward of any expectations of inheriting the property and had told Merrilee that the house was to be sold and the proceeds sent to a missionary church, she had not revealed that this was not to happen until Merrilee graduated from high school. Until that time she was to stay in the house.

Brother John, Willadean's much admired preacher

and church leader, had promptly challenged her wish, claiming that at sixteen Merrilee was too young to live alone. The thought of moving in with him and his wife, Sister Bridie, had so appalled Merrilee that she'd plucked up her courage to speak privately with the judge. He had listened to all her arguments but kept probing until she had to admit the truth. With equal amounts of embarrassment, shame, and guilt, she had haltingly told him that the preacher used the pretext of kneeling in prayer to put his arm around her. It wasn't a gesture that seemed fatherly to her, especially when he wedged himself so tightly against her that the back of his hand rubbed against her breast and his thigh pressed hotly against hers.

In retrospect Merrilee realized what a gamble her visit to Judge Cramer had been. He could have accused her of being hysterical, of misunderstanding the preacher, of impugning his reputation. He had done none of those things. He had listened intently. Then he had allowed her to use her Social Security allotment to live in the house with a weekly visit by Sister Bridie to inspect the premises. To this day, Merrilee was grateful to Judge Cramer for his unorthodox decision.

Merrilee pulled into the Oak Street driveway, where she sat for several minutes just looking at the house. Except for needing a coat of paint, it seemed unchanged. The deep front porch where she had spent many summer evenings listening to and singing along with Patsy Cline, Joan Baez, and Joni Mitchell looked as inviting as ever. A lump rose in her throat. Though it was only a modest two-bedroom frame house, it was the only home she had ever known. Her life before moving here was a vague but terrifying memory of institutions. After she had left, the years had blurred into a series of indistinguishable motel rooms and tour buses.

When her eyes misted, Merrilee wiped them guiltily, recalling Willadean's fist rule of life: "Don't bawl. It's a waste of time and energy." If there was one thing her guardian couldn't be accused of, it was wasting either.

Inside, the house smelled of dust, mice, and mildew. In the empty rooms the scarred wooden floors, the threadbare rugs, and the loose, stained, faded wallpaper spoke of years of neglect. Merrilee walked slowly through the rooms, opening all the windows. When she unstuck the last kitchen window, she jumped back with a startled cry.

"I didn't mean to scare you," the elderly woman standing outside said. Craning her neck for a closer look, she asked, "Merrilee? Is that you? Well, mercy on me. It *is* you. I'd recognize that fiery hair of yours anywhere."

Merrilee studied the seamed, smiling face. "Mrs. Farmer?"

"You remember me! I knew you would, no matter how famous you got."

Merrilee unlocked the back door for the woman who'd been her neighbor, co-worker, and ally. She couldn't begin to number the times Peggy Farmer had sided with her in trying to change Willadean's rigid, outdated ideas of raising a young girl. Peggy hadn't changed much in the intervening years. Her short-legged body had put on a few more pounds around her ample hips, her hair was grayer, but she still wore the kind of outfits she'd worn for as long as Merrilee could remember: elastic-waisted polyester slacks with a matching smock-style top.

"Please come in." Merrilee smiled at the woman warmly. They hugged. "How are you?"

"Pretty tolerable, thanks. No need to ask how you are," Peggy said, peering nearsightedly up into Merrilee's face. "You look so pretty. Who'd have thought that when Willadean led that scrawny six-year-old into this house, you'd turn into a beauty? You were all big, scared, blue eyes and tangled, wavy hair halfway down your back. Willadean and me must have spent an hour untangling, combing, and braiding your mane. I know it must have hurt, but you never even whimpered. I said to Willadean, I did, that she'd got herself a tough little fighter."

No, she hadn't, Merrilee reflected. All she'd gotten was a little girl too terrified to complain or cry, lest the woman take her back to the orphanage.

"What are you doing here?" Peggy asked.

"I bought the house."

"Well, don't that beat all. As an investment?" Peggy looked around the old-fashioned, shabby kitchen skeptically.

"No, I'm going to live here."

"Why, of course. Your aunt finally got a hold of you, and you came back to be with her. I should have known."

"My aunt?"

"Yeah, Hazel. Your mother's only sister. She's out to the Maple Lane Nursing Home." Studying the young woman's face, Peggy exclaimed, "You didn't know? Her messages never reached you?"

"No. I've been touring for the past six months."

"Well, won't Hazel be surprised."

No more surprised than she was, Merrilee mused. "When did Hazel get back from India or wherever she was?"

"About seven months ago. She's a widow woman now. You're the only kin she's got."

"That didn't mean a thing to her in the past."

"I don't think that's so," Peggy, ever softhearted, protested.

"Yes, it is. When I was sixteen, I found the letter she wrote in reply to the news that her sister had died in a fire, leaving a four-year-old girl. She wrote that she was too busy with her missionary work, and didn't Kentucky have good, Christian institutions to take care of an orphan?"

"Well, I'm sure she didn't mean—"

"Yes, she did. For years I dreamed that she'd send for me, that I'd sail off on a big ocean liner and help her convert all those little heathen children she cared so much about. But she never even sent a Christmas card, not once. So why should I go see her now?"

"But she's your only living kin!"

"That meant nothing to her then. It means nothing to me now."

"You've grown hard, Merrilee."

"Maybe so, but it's a hard, cold world." Seeing the disappointment in Peggy's faded eyes, Merrilee changed the subject. Glancing around, she said, "Looks like I'll have my work cut out for me. The house is really run-down."

"Them sorry no-accounts that bought it couldn't be bothered with a lick of painting or repairing. I was mighty relieved when they left. It'll be like old times, having you back."

"Are you still working at Browne's Emporium?"

"Naw. I retired last year. My legs are too poorly for all that standing behind the checkout counter. And Mr. Roth retired three years ago. The store ain't nearly as nice a place to work at now as it was when we were there together."

Merrilee remembered the store primarily for the long hours she'd put in there every day after school since her freshman year. "Are you enjoying being a lady of leisure?"

"Sure am. Say, I could help you with the house. You know, tell you about the best carpenters, electricians, and such."

"Thank you. That would be a great help."

"Are you spending the night here?"

"No. The utilities haven't been turned on yet. I'm staying at the Holiday Inn out by the bypass."

Peggy turned toward the back door. "I'd better go and start Howard's supper. He gets grumpy if the food ain't on the table the minute he gets home."

"How's Howard?"

Peggy grinned. "As tough as white leather and as independent as a hog on ice."

Merrilee chuckled. "In other words, he hasn't changed."

"Nope. There's been many a day when I wished he would, but I reckon that won't happen in this life."

"Seems to me that for as long as you've stuck with him, you must like him the way he is."

"You're right, but don't let on to him about that. Say, why don't you come for supper?"

"Thanks, I'd love to, but I still have a couple of appointments this afternoon. Can I take a rain check?"

"Sure. Anytime."

"You still bake your own pies?"

"Yeah. Your favorites were blackberry and cherry, right?"

"I haven't tasted anything that good since I left here."

"Call me when you want to come, and I'll bake you a pie. That's a promise. Make it soon. I know Howard'll want to see you too. He's a real fan of your singing, but then, he always was."

Merrilee walked Peggy to the kitchen door.

"I'm glad you're back." With a parting smile, Peggy left. When she reached her back porch, she turned. Seeing Merrilee still standing inside the screen door, she called out, "Think about visiting your aunt. She's old and lonely. I'm sure she would appreciate seeing you."

Merrilee waved back. Learning that her aunt was in Browne's Station had been a shock. She had never dreamed the woman would come back to the town she had left some thirty years ago. Maybe she would visit Hazel. Just out of curiosity. Merrilee was probably the least sentimental person she knew. Willadean's teachings had seen to that.

Chapter Two

Five days after Merrilee moved into the Oak Street house, the letter arrived. It was short and to the point:

You don't belong here. Leave.

The one-line message was embellished with a crude drawing, showing a male stick figure aiming a hand-gun at a female stick figure.

Merrilee dropped the sheet of paper onto the card table she'd set up in the kitchen. A shiver of apprehension shook her. This was stupid. The note was only a prank. Then why did it make her skin crawl and her mouth go dry? She glanced uneasily at the lengthening shadows in the backyard. Very soon, too soon, it would be dark.

On tour it was standard procedure to report all threats against the band's members to local authorities. It would be foolish to do anything less now. Before she could argue herself out of it, she picked up the phone and dialed 911.

While she waited for the promised patrol car, she tried to keep herself busy making mental lists of what needed to be done.

Besides the card table and chairs in the kitchen, Merrilee had bought a set of mattresses and window shades for her upstairs bedroom. She would acquire furniture after the rooms were painted and wallpapered and the floors sanded. The one thing she had really needed was a piano. She was lucky to have found an old walnut upright that had been painstakingly restored. Running her fingers over the keyboard, she thought that she had probably paid too much for it, but she'd fallen in love with the instrument instantly. It reminded her of the one that used to stand in the same spot when she'd been a girl.

Willadean had taught her the basic piano techniques, claiming it was a waste of good money to pay someone else to do it. When Merrilee surpassed her teacher's skills within six months, Willadean, in an unprecedented turnabout, had hired a professional teacher. Though she never explained her reasons, she always managed to be present during the piano lessons. In retrospect, Merrilee wondered if deep down Willadean had yearned for additional training. It would have been characteristic of her to think it frivolous and self-indulgent for a grown woman to take lessons.

The sound of the doorbell echoed loudly through the empty rooms. Merrilee hurried to the door. When she saw a tall, khaki-uniformed policeman standing on the porch, she unlocked the screen door.

"Miss Ingram?"

Merrilee nodded. "Please come in."

"I'm Quentin Garner, chief of police. The dispatcher said you had a problem."

His rank took her aback. "Nothing serious enough to warrant a visit from the chief of police," she protested.

"In Browne's Station that rank doesn't mean a whole lot. You got me because the deputy on evening duty is eating supper. What can I do for you?"

"I received a 'get out of Dodge' letter."

Chief Garner took off his mirrored sunglasses. "Are you serious?"

"Yes. The letter's back in the kitchen." Merrilee led the way. "Here it is."

When she started to pick it up, he said, "Don't. I realize you've touched it already, but the less it's handled, the better our chances of lifting prints."

"Do you think the sender would have been so careless as to leave fingerprints after going to the trouble of pretending he or she is a child by printing like a first-grader?"

"Probably not, but it's best not to take chances."

While he studied the note, Merrilee studied him. She guessed him to be in his mid-thirties with his fine blond hair cut by a barber, not a stylist. His face was rather ordinary except for his mouth, which made her think of Jim Morrison of The Doors. It had that same sensuous-cruel look she always found so appealing.

When he looked up, she knew she'd been wrong. There was nothing ordinary about his eyes.

"You're right. This wasn't printed by a child. Did this note arrive in the mail?"

"Yes. The envelope is under the note."

The chief took a pen from his pocket and used it to flip the business-sized envelope right side up.

"It's postmarked Browne's Station. I agree with you that there are probably no useful prints, but we should be able to identify the typewriter model used to type the address. That might be helpful later on. Do you often get this kind of mail?"

Merrilee shrugged. "The group's gotten bad fan mail from time to time. It goes with the territory. I'm a singer," she added in explanation.

"I know who you are, Miss Ingram."

"Oh."

"Let's see. You arrived one week ago today."

"How come you know the exact date?"

"My secretary went to high school with you. Her sister works at the Holiday Inn, recognized you . . . Well, surely you remember how fast news spreads in a small town."

"Yes, 'like a good case of pinkeye,' Willadean used to say. She's the woman who raised me." Realizing that this sort of information was irrelevant, she changed the subject quickly. "I wouldn't have bothered to report this except that the drawing . . ." Merrilee shivered. "The message itself isn't that scary, but the drawing gives me the willies."

Using his pen, the chief eased the letter and the envelope into a small plastic bag. "The drawing adds menace. Whoever sent this knew it would. When the next letter comes, try to touch it as little as possible."

"You think there will be more?"

"Don't you?"

"Yes." Merrilee couldn't have pinpointed her reasons for thinking there would be more letters, but on a purely visceral level she was convinced of it. Hugging her arms around her waist, she watched Quentin Garner examine the lock on her back door. With a frown he wrote something in his notebook.

"I wrote down the name and number of a reliable locksmith. I want you to call him and have him install decent locks on all exterior doors." He tore the sheet out of the notebook and handed it to Merrilee.

"What about tonight?"

"You'll be okay. If someone meant to harm you tonight, they wouldn't have bothered sending the letter. Do you have old enemies here?"

Merrilee stared at him speechlessly. Finally she asked, "Are you serious? I left twelve years ago."

"Some people hold grudges forever. You've got to realize that people who send these kinds of letters aren't exactly normal. Think back. Did anything unusual happen just before you left?"

She thought for a couple of seconds before shaking her head. "No. At least I don't remember anything. I'd quit my job the day before graduation. After the ceremony, I went next door to have dinner with the Farmers. Later that evening I attended Heather Cunningham's party but stayed only a short time because I still had packing to do. The next morning I caught the early bus to Lexington."

"You haven't been back since?"

"No."

"Did you stay in touch with anyone here?"

"At first I wrote to Mrs. Farmer, but she's not much of a correspondent, so I quit except for Christmas cards. I never got in touch with anyone until I wrote to Sam Stewart about buying this house. It can't be anything that goes that far back."

"You think it's connected to your singing career?"

"It's the only thing that makes any sense. I mean, it doesn't really, but there are crazies out there who love to threaten entertainers. It doesn't seem to matter whether we sing country, pop, rock, soul, the blues, or whatever. We all get crank mail."

"As I said before, I don't think you're in any immediate danger, but lock all your doors and windows. Leave the outside lights on all night. I'll have a patrol car drive by several times. Call immediately when you get another letter, and don't handle it."

Merrilee nodded. When he opened the front door, she noticed that night had fallen. Her heart skipped a beat.

Almost as if he'd sensed her reaction, the chief said, "If you're uneasy about staying here alone, why don't you check into the Holiday Inn for the night?"

"No. I won't let this weirdo drive me out of my own home. Besides, aren't most of these letter-writers harmless?" He hesitated to speak, so she read the unpalatable truth in his expression. "As you said, I should be all right tonight, and I'll get better locks tomorrow. Thank you for coming."

"Lock the door behind me. I'll call you tomorrow."

That didn't sound like something a lawman would say. On the other hand, Quentin Garner didn't look like the stereotypical southern small-town redneck lawman either. When she heard the patrol car drive off, she felt a twinge of panic. It suddenly occurred to her that the curtainless living room windows exposed her to whatever was out there in the dark as if she were on a lighted stage. Quickly she turned off all the lights and ran upstairs. She could work on the lyrics to a song she was composing just as easily in her bedroom. The only problem was, she couldn't concentrate. At eleven she gave up and went to bed.

In sleep she battled her old nightmare again, for the first time in years. When she awoke at four in the morning, wet with perspiration, her heart pounding, she jumped out of bed. Nothing on earth would have induced her to go back to sleep and risk experiencing that terror again. Watching the world wake up, she tried again to remember what had frightened her so, but she couldn't. She never could.

The next day Chief Garner arrived a few minutes before the mailman was due to turn the corner into Oak Street. Again he wore aviator-style reflector glasses, which he kept on while they waited on the porch. Merrilee surprised herself by wanting him to take them off so she could see his startlingly green eyes again. She wondered why he kept them on.

She usually wore dark glasses when she signed autographs for fans during afternoon performances because they offered her a little privacy, a little protection from the strangers who thought they knew her from her songs and therefore had a personal claim on her. While she thought she had a reason for wearing them, she could not guess why this lawman found it necessary to hide behind lenses so dark that no eye could penetrate them. Did he have to look at human misdeeds so horrendous that they could be viewed only obliquely? Probably.

Merrilee sat in the porch swing. Quentin Garner stood with one black boot propped on the porch railing, the fingertips of his hands stuck into the back pockets of his khakis. He was a quiet man, reserved, or so he appeared to her, since he didn't find it necessary to indulge in small talk.

According to Peggy, he was single and lived by himself in a small house. That's all Peggy knew with certainty, though she mentioned the rumors that had him driving to Lexington once or twice a month. To visit a girlfriend? If so, then it was not exactly a red-hot romance. But then, Merrilee was hardly an expert on matters of the heart, even though her songs dealt largely with male-female relationships.

Music from the radio floated through the open living room window. The male vocalist sang in the traditional through-the-nose country style, pure twang accompanied by whining steel guitars, pleading to be left alone to live his life his way, to seek oblivion through whiskey and drugs. Merrilee hated songs like that. They reminded her of her lead guitarist, Hap Jensen, who lived just like that, never mind the worry and pain he inflicted on those around him.

"Here comes the mailman." Quentin took his foot off the railing and sat next to Merrilee. "No sense in tipping him off," he said, laying his arm along the back of the swing. That lent a deceptive intimacy to the scene.

"Aren't you afraid of starting rumors?"

He turned his head to look at her. "How?"

"With your arm behind my shoulders, the casual observer might be misled into thinking your visit is personal rather than official."

"That's what I want them to think. Do you mind?"

"Good heavens, no! After all the garbage the tabloids have written about me? About my engagement? I've grown a thick skin."

"I don't read the tabloids."

He looked at her as if he wanted her to elaborate. "I was engaged to Hank Corian, and we did break up. That much is true. But the tabloids added all sorts of stuff to inject drama and spice. I briefly considered a lawsuit, but that probably would have kept us in the headlines even longer."

"On what terms did you part with Corian? How did he take your leaving?"

"Let's just say that the fit he pitched was extreme even for him." Merrilee was silent for a moment before she spoke. "If you're thinking that Hank had anything to do with this note, you're wrong. I left him over four years ago."

"From all accounts the man's got an ego the size of the national debt. He wouldn't take kindly to a woman's walking out on him. Didn't he threaten to ruin your career?"

"Yes, but that was anger and liquor talking. He's had several lovers since then. And my career is going fine. Do you find it difficult to believe that someone local sent this note?"

"Not at all. I'm just trying to narrow down the possibilities."

The postman greeted them, trying not to eye them too obviously while he stuffed the mail into the box screwed to the wall beside the front door. After he left, Quentin removed the mail with a handkerchief-covered hand. However, there was no threatening letter among the junk mail addressed to Occupant.

"I'll be back in time to look at tomorrow's mail. Your new lock looks good," he said, nodding toward the front door.

"The locksmith came right after I phoned him. Thanks for talking to him." Merrilee stayed on the porch until Quentin drove off.

That evening Merrilee joined the Farmers for supper.

No sooner had Peggy placed the last bowl of food on the table and slid into her chair than she started on the topic she'd been dying to discuss.

"Abe said he seen you and Quentin Garner sitting on the porch. Looked like courtin' to him."

Merrilee's hands froze on the bowl she was in the process of passing to Howard. "News gets around even faster than I thought. Who's Abe?"

"The mailman. So, it's true?"

"That he was on my porch, yes. That he was courting me, no."

"Then what was he doing sitting with you on your porch?"

"Peggy, maybe that ain't none of your business. Pass the okra, please." Howard held out a hand for the bowl.

"Sorry." Merrilee passed him the bowl, trying to decide what she should tell them.

"Well, Merrilee could do a whole lot worse than Quentin Garner. He's got a steady job, a good reputation, and even though he ain't as handsome as Hank Corian, he ain't homely neither. Don't you think so?" Peggy asked Merrilee.

"No, he isn't homely."

"You ain't still hung up on that Hank Corian, are you?"

"No, Peggy, I'm not."

"Good. From what I read about him, he's as drunk as a skunk at a moonshine still more often than not. You were smart to get rid of him."

Peggy took a bite from her hush puppy, and Merrilee breathed easier. Perhaps she had forgotten about Quentin's reason for being on her porch. "This catfish is delicious."

"It's all in getting the grease the right temperature. So, why was the police chief sitting with you?"

Merrilee had forgotten what a one-track mind Peggy had. After a brief mental struggle she decided to tell them the truth. If she couldn't trust these two people whom she had known for most of her life, she was in serious trouble.

"I received a threatening letter in the mail. It told me to get out of town because I didn't belong here. I called the police department, and Chief Garner came." Forks stopped in midair. Two pairs of rounded eyes stared at her in mute amazement.

"Mercy me! So that's why you had new locks put on your doors."

"You got a gun?" Howard asked.

"No."

"You'd better take one of mine."

"I haven't shot a gun since you took me to target practice when I was twelve," Merrilee protested.

"It's something you don't forget. Like riding a bicycle." Having recovered from his shock, Howard took another piece of fish.

"I don't have a gun permit."

Howard looked at her in disbelief. "Everybody's got guns around here. Unless you carry it on your person, nobody's going to check for a permit."

Even though she'd handled a gun years ago, Merrilee wasn't comfortable having one in her house. The idea of aiming it at another human being appalled her.

Sensing her reluctance, Howard added, "Use it to signal. You know, if you hear something in the night, aim the gun at the ceiling and squeeze the trigger. I'll hear it and come running."

"What's the chief doing about this letter?" Peggy asked.

"We're waiting for another letter."

"That's all?"

"The chief knows his business," Howard said. "He's got the training, and he comes from an educated family."

"Howard, how do you know that?" Peggy demanded.

Merrilee thought Howard looked as if he wished he'd never uttered a word.

"You may as well tell me right off," Peggy said, stabbing a finger in his direction for emphasis. "You know I'll get it out of you sooner or later." Peggy refilled his glass with tea. She waited until he had drained half the tea before she prompted, "Well? We're waiting. How'd you learn about Quentin's family?"

Howard sighed in defeat. "One of the boys I work with is from Lexington. He knows of the Garners. Quentin's daddy teaches at the university."

"Land's sake, Howard, go on!"

"There ain't much more to tell. Quentin served a tour of duty in the Middle East somewhere, and I think the guy said he'd been married."

"Every woman in town knows he doesn't have a wife now." Peggy leaned toward her husband. "Try to remember exactly what was said."

"Is this important?"

Peggy looked at Merrilee and shook her head pityingly. "Men," she muttered. "Of course, it's important."

Howard scratched his chest where the buttons of his shirt strained over his spare tire. "As close as I can recollect, he said Quentin got married after he got out of the service. His wife passed away some years ago."

"A widower," Peggy said, her voice filled with sympathy. "That's mighty interesting."

Fearing her neighbor was plotting a romantic encounter for her and the chief, Merrilee couldn't think of any distraction other than offering to help with the dishes.

"Okay. I'll wash, and you dry."

At least for the moment Peggy's mind was on other matters. That lasted until they'd finished the dishes and she slid pieces of blackberry pie onto plates.

"What kind of pie do you suppose he likes?"

Howard exchanged a puzzled look with Merrilee. "You know dang well what kind of pies I like. Ought to after forty years of marriage."

"Not you. Quentin."

"What difference does that make to you?" Howard asked.

"The graveyard cleaning's coming up. He always helps. I thought we could invite him to eat with us and Merrilee. Is that okay with y'all?"

Howard merely grunted. Merrilee said, "You still have an annual cleanup?"

"We still got a graveyard, ain't we?" Peggy squinted at the wall, mulling over the pie dilemma. "I'll bake three kinds. That way we're bound to have one he'll like. I'll do one sweet potato pie. Men always like sweet potato. Must be that half cup of whiskey that's in it."

After they'd finished eating dessert, Howard insisted they all gather around the old family organ and sing songs as they had in the past.

"That was mighty nice. I always enjoyed that. Now let me show you my guns." Howard unlocked the old-fashioned chifforobe and proudly displayed his arsenal.

Howard owned a half dozen handguns, each of which he had to show to Merrilee. He extolled the virtues of each enthusiastically. Since she knew he would not let her leave without a weapon, Merrilee chose a Colt, the very gun he had used to teach her to shoot cans off a fence.

"I never cottoned to guns much," Peggy said.

"I'm not crazy about them either, but there are times they might come in handy."

Merrilee loaded the Colt under Howard's supervision.

Gun in hand, she walked the short distance separating the back doors of the two houses. Merrilee had left the outside lights on. Odd, she thought, walking up the back steps. She couldn't remember a rope hanging over the back door. Suddenly the end of the rope curled up. Inches from her face the mouth opened, its tongue shooting toward her. Mesmerized, Merrilee stared into two deadly, glittering eyes.

Chapter Three

"**A**re you feeling any better?" Peggy asked, bending over Merrilee, who sat hunched on the piano bench in the living room.

Merrilee nodded weakly. She closed her eyes tightly against the sickening sight that seemed to be imprinted on her retinas.

Even though she didn't really want anything, Merrilee knew it would make Peggy feel better if she could perform some small service. "Maybe a glass of water would help," she said. After her neighbor had hurried off in the direction of the kitchen, Merrilee concentrated on breathing deeply. She prayed she wouldn't fall apart and cry.

A couple of minutes later Peggy returned with Howard and Quentin, who had been out on the back porch, examining the snake.

"You sure you don't want something a little stronger?

I can get you a shot of fine sipping whiskey," Howard offered.

"No, thanks. Water is fine." Merrilee sipped cautiously, not knowing if she could keep it down. Mercifully her stomach accepted the water. Seeing the three people standing around her, she said, "I'm sorry there's nowhere for you to sit."

"Don't worry about that," Peggy said.

Quentin hunkered down in front of her. "Tell me exactly what happened. From the beginning."

His voice was low, soothing, yet resonant and reminded her of the timbre of a fine bass guitar. By concentrating on the memory of the beguiling sound of a bass guitar, she held the ugly image of the snake at bay.

"There isn't much to tell. I came home from Peggy and Howard's after supper. At first I thought it was strange that there was a rope hanging from the ceiling of the back porch. Until I came closer." Merrilee stopped, unable to continue.

"The copperhead didn't bite you?"

"I guess I wasn't quite close enough for that." Merrilee took another sip of water. "I must have screamed. At least that's what Peggy said; she heard me from her kitchen. She and Howard came running. Howard had lent me a gun. He pried it from my hand and shot the snake."

"Blew that sucker's head clean off." Howard hitched up his gray twill pants, pleased with himself.

"Then we came inside, and Howard phoned you." Merrilee thought for a moment. "What I don't understand is how the snake got up there. Howard said it was a copperhead. I thought they lived in woods and rocky areas."

"They do. That snake didn't crawl up there by it-self."

Merrilee looked at Quentin searchingly. "Are you saying someone put it there?"

Quentin nodded.

Merrilee swayed. In an instant Peggy was on the bench beside her, one arm around her, holding her up-right.

Quentin took the glass from Merrilee and set it on the floor. He placed his hand on hers. "Are you okay?"

"I don't know. I've never had someone hang a poi-sonous snake over my door before."

"If'n the copperhead don't strike you in the head, the bite ain't usually fatal to a grown-up," Howard in-formed her.

"Well, that's hardly the point," Peggy said, and she shot Howard a disapproving look, her free hand tuck-ing a strand of her untidy, permed hair behind her ear. "They're snakes, and snakes are nasty critters. They give me the creeps."

"Why would someone do this?" Merrilee asked, hurt and puzzled.

"I don't know. Could be part of the campaign to get you out of town started by the letter-writer. We've checked the doors and the windows. They're secure. Nobody attempted to enter or slipped a snake into the house. You should be safe."

Quentin felt the shudder that rippled through Mer-rilee. He tightened his hand around hers. Then he looked at Peggy and at Howard, who'd positioned himself beside his wife.

"Did either of you glance out your window tonight? Notice anyone hanging around Merrilee's house?"

"I don't remember looking out." Howard shrugged, obviously sorry he was missing his chance to help the chief.

"You want to spend the night in our spare room?" Peggy asked.

"Thanks. I admit I'm tempted, but I can't let this person drive me out. I'll be all right."

Quentin looked at Merrilee. "I'll walk Peggy and Howard to the door and lock it behind them. Okay?"

Merrilee nodded. When he returned, she glanced at him again fearfully.

"My deputy took the snake with him."

Her relief was almost palpable. "Thanks. I didn't want to find it on the step in the morning." She was silent until she forced herself to think logically of the night's events. "What I don't understand is, who would want to handle a dangerous snake? I mean, they must have caught it and somehow put it up there. That takes a lot of touching." Revulsion coursed through Merrilee. "Who would want to do that?"

"There are people who handle poisonous snakes as a profession. They gather the venom for medical clinics. Some religious groups used them as part of their ceremonies until the practice was outlawed, but every so often I hear rumors that some factions still use them occasionally. And then there are some people who simply like to mess with snakes."

Merrilee shook her head. "I can't imagine doing that."

"I can't either."

"I suppose the snake is as much a dead end as the letter."

"I wouldn't say that. Tomorrow I'll make some inquiries. There can't be that many snake fanatics in Browne's Station. I also have the netting used to suspend the copperhead from the ceiling. That's enough to get started on. Now, if you're okay, I'll get going."

"I'm all right." Merrilee wasn't as certain of that as she sounded, but she was used to taking care of herself and her problems. She had been doing that for a long, long time.

Quentin held out a hand to help Merrilee up from the piano bench. He kept a firm grasp on her elbow until they reached the front door. "Lock the door behind me. I'll look in on you again tomorrow."

Merrilee gazed into his light green eyes, and for a moment she was tempted to ask him to stay. She quickly squelched the impulse. It was a crazy idea, alien to her careful nature. Quentin would probably decline on the grounds that it would be unprofessional or that he had a lover in Lexington. If he didn't reject the invitation, things might get out of hand, and that would be even worse.

Subconsciously she'd sensed that coming back to Browne's Station formed a watershed in her life. To complicate this by becoming lovers with a relative stranger would be insane, impulsive, irrational. Merrilee couldn't remember ever contemplating, much less committing, such a rash act before. So she simply said, "Thank you for all you've done," and watched him leave. She turned the key in the lock.

A sudden creaking from near the top of the stairs caused her heart to leap into her throat. She reminded herself that this was an old house. Old houses, like old people, creaked.

She gave herself a little pep talk. "Okay, Merrilee Ingram, show what you're made of. You are a strong woman. You can do this." Feeling more confident, she sat down at the piano and started to pound the keys. She played Strauss waltzes spiritedly, their buoyant beat and gaiety defying her unknown tormentor to come and face her. No one came.

The next morning the whole world seemed determined to distract her. On his way to the cardboard-box manufacturing plant where he worked, Howard stopped in to check on her. Along with the noisy painters, a representative from the building-supply store arrived. Merrilee spent three hours selecting ceramic tiles for the bathrooms and the kitchen. When she felt unable to make even one more decision, she asked the salesman to leave the sample books with her.

At noon Peggy arrived, carrying a covered plate.

"Brought you a ham sandwich," she announced, searching Merrilee's face anxiously. "I'd have come sooner, but Howard said you was okay and to leave you be for a while."

Accepting the plate, Merrilee thanked her.

"What are you doing this afternoon?" Peggy wanted to know.

Merrilee looked at the stack of sample books. "I'm supposed to pick out wallpaper." She sighed.

"That's the last thing you want to do, right?"

"Right."

"Why don't you go visit your aunt out at the Maple Lane Nursing Home? I know how you feel," Peggy said, forestalling Merrilee's protests, "but I also know a visit with your aunt would do you some good too."

Merrilee looked at the angle of Peggy's chin and shook her head. "I'd forgotten how stubborn you can be once you get a bee in your bonnet, as Willadean used to say. In the first place, I don't even know where this nursing home is, and in the second, I don't know their visiting hours. So I couldn't go, even if I were so inclined." Merrilee was pleased with her cogently presented reasons.

"Maple Lane is just east of the highway. You can't miss the nursing home. It used to be the old Sleepy Time Motel. They allow visitors right after dinner and again after supper." With a self-satisfied expression Peggy drew her shapeless cardigan together and folded her arms underneath her matronly bosom.

"You think you've got this all figured out, don't you? You imagine this big, tearful family reconciliation and reunion. Well, I doubt that will happen. Hazel Jones Peterson could pass me on the street and not know me. Besides, she's probably not any more eager to meet me than I am to see her."

"That's where you're dead wrong. Hazel wants to meet you in the worst way, and she'd recognize you in a flash. She's got one of your CDs with your picture on it."

"How do you know that?"

"I met her." Peggy clearly enjoyed Merrilee's astonishment. "When she first came back, she called around, trying to locate you. Somebody told her you used to live here on Oak Street. She came knocking on my door, and we got to talking over a glass of iced tea."

"Did you now? And you two decided that she and I should meet. Just like that." Peggy's smugness was beginning to grate on Merrilee.

"What could be more natural? After all, blood's thicker than water. There's nothing more important than family."

Merrilee had forgotten the southern small-town preoccupation with family, where a common gene pool overruled all other considerations.

Sensing a weakening in Merrilee's resolve, Peggy changed tactics. "Why don't you sit down and eat your sandwich and relax. You don't have to make a decision about visiting Hazel right this minute. Just think about it." Without waiting for a rejoinder, Peggy scooted out the back door.

Merrilee stared resentfully after Peggy until the aroma of smoked ham rising from the plate distracted her. Since she hadn't felt up to anything more than a cup of strong black coffee earlier, her stomach growled hungrily. Uncovering the plate, she discovered a generously filled, fist-sized biscuit.

She closed her eyes blissfully as she chewed the first bite, for the biscuit was as light and flaky as she remembered. Peggy probably still used lard, which probably clogged her arteries even as she ate. Well, she might not live long enough for it to matter whether her arteries were clogged or not.

Startled, she realized that this was the first time she'd consciously admitted to herself that she might be in a life-threatening situation. Mulling this over, she thought again of the unresolved matter of her will or, rather, the lack of one. Her logical beneficiaries would be the members of her band. They'd been together for ten years and were the closest thing to a family she'd had. Yet she hesitated.

They'd go on a mammoth party spree that would end only with their arrest or hospitalization. Or their deaths. Leaving money to the three men she loved like brothers would be the worst thing she could do for them.

That left Peggy and Howard. As long as she had blood relatives, they would be truly shocked and uncomfortable if she bequeathed the bulk of her estate to them. That left Hazel. Drat Peggy for telling her about her aunt.

Merrilee found herself wondering about the woman much too frequently. She also knew that Peggy would keep nagging her until she visited Hazel. The woman never gave up. Merrilee dashed upstairs to change her clothes.

It would only be a brief duty call, she assured herself as she parked her car in front of the nursing home.

She sat there a minute, studying the building in front of her. Although some effort had been made to disguise its former function, the basic structure of the building revealed its motel beginnings.

The interior space of the squared off U-shape of the motel, which had housed the swimming pool, had been filled in and roofed over.

Inside, the area was divided by movable six-foot-high partitions, which formed a small lobby with a recreation area behind it. The odor that assailed Merrilee was that of lemon-scented, ammonia-based household cleaner. Underneath this powerful odor she detected the harsh smell of some other unknown, slightly frightening scent. Did hopelessness have a scent?

"Can I help you?" the big, rawboned, middle-aged woman behind the lobby counter asked.

Except it sounded like *kin I hep you.* Although the woman wore what looked like a nurse's scrubs, she lacked a badge identifying her as such.

"I'd like to see Mrs. Hazel Peterson, please."

"Are you a relation?"

"Yes. I'm her niece." Merrilee found herself being examined by cool eyes that shrewdly calculated the cost of her outfit and the simple gold-and-pearl earrings she wore.

"I'm Mrs. Gladys Vernon. My husband is the manager of this little haven for our sweet old dears. I'm so glad to meet you. Mrs. Peterson's such an uncomplaining angel, even though she's had so few visitors in the time she's been with us."

Mrs. Vernon's sugary voice managed to combine

slight condemnation with the promise of future approval if the offending behavior was suitably and swiftly altered.

"I returned to town only a few days ago. How's my aunt?"

"Who can tell?" Gladys shrugged her beefy shoulders. "She's such a patient, God-fearing, self-sacrificing soul, it's hard to say when she needs something and is too shy or too frugal to ask for it."

She directed her eyes heavenward, which elongated her rather long neck even more. With her build, the long neck did not lend her a swanlike grace. Rather, it made her look a bit like a plump vulture.

"Can you please direct me to her room?"

"*Her* room?" Gladys tried to suppress the smirk that threatened her composure.

The smirk annoyed Merrilee.

"Her pension from the missionary board doesn't allow her a room to herself. She's sharing it with another lady."

"Then will you direct me to this room she's sharing?" Merrilee asked with enough steel in her voice to brook no further delay. "Mrs. Vernon, what's your function in this nursing home?"

"I'm the assistant manager and a licensed practical nurse," Gladys answered with considerable pride.

Glancing at the hefty upper arms that strained the short sleeves of her uniform, Merrilee thought the staff undoubtedly called for Gladys when one of their "sweet old dears" got out of line.

"I'll show you where your aunt is."

Gladys opened the door to room twelve without knocking. The only difference Merrilee could see between this room and a hospital room was that it contained a couple of extra chairs.

"Your aunt is over by the window."

As soon as the patient nearest the door heard the assistant manager's voice, she started talking nonstop to the apparently elusive Gladys. The patient launched into a long list of complaints and demands.

Merrilee's aunt lay on her side, facing the tightly shut window, ignoring the loud voice of her roommate. Merrilee walked around the bed and sat in the visitor's chair.

"Aunt Hazel?" The woman's mauve-toned eyelids fluttered faintly but remained closed. Merrilee tried desperately to find something familiar in the thin figure, something that reminded her of herself, of the blood ties between them, but couldn't.

Hazel's hair was white, her skin so thin and lined that it looked like a crumpled tissue. Doing some quick mental arithmetic, Merrilee decided that Hazel's age had to be somewhere around seventy, even though she looked years older than that. The missionary life she'd led in those far-off places had been hard on her. Suddenly Merrilee found herself strangely intrigued by that life.

"Aunt Hazel?"

This time the eyes fluttered open. They were curiously unfocused, the pupils much too large. Merrilee recognized that spaced-out downers' look and hated it. She'd seen it in too many musicians' eyes to mistake it for anything but what it was. Hazel was drugged. Was this done routinely here?

"Reba? Reba honey, is that you?"

"No, Aunt Hazel, this is Merrilee. Reba's daughter."

"Reba's girl?"

"Yes."

Hazel's voice was faint, the words carefully formed as she struggled against the effect of the sedative.

"Your hair." A lengthy pause followed. "Reba . . . not red."

That was a surprise. Merrilee always figured she'd inherited her hair color from her mother.

"Aunt Hazel?" Merrilee gently shook the bony shoulder under the thin, faded cotton gown. "Aunt Hazel?" There was no response. The sedative had overpowered Hazel. "I'll be back," she promised the still figure.

With determined steps Merrilee strode to the front desk. "Where is Mrs. Vernon?" she asked the gum-chewing young woman placing papers into a filing cabinet.

"She was called in to help with a patient."

"Tell her that Merrilee Ingram will be back tomorrow and wants to see the medical file on her aunt. Got that?"

The young woman's eyes rounded in surprise. "Yes'm," she said, and she popped her gum.

All the way back to Oak Street Merrilee kept thinking about Hazel. She was so preoccupied, she absent-mindedly accepted the stack of mail from the postman, whom she met in front of her house. She placed it on the wrought-iron table next to the front entrance while she unlocked the door.

The top letters slid off an oversized, glossy card on the bottom. Merrilee jumped back with an exclamation of loathing. The photograph had captured the brilliant colors of a coiled snake. Shaking with revulsion, she flipped the card over.

The message on the reverse side caused her to back away in terror.

Chapter Four

Merrilee kept walking backward, her eyes riveted on the crude drawing on the back of the card, until she bumped into something solid. With a small cry of alarm, she whirled around.

"Easy. It's just me." Seeing the panic in her eyes, Quentin gently placed his hands on her shoulders. "Take it easy. It'll be okay." A little of the panic in her eyes faded, but her shoulders remained rigid with tension.

"What happened?" he demanded. Realizing how official he sounded, Quentin repeated the question in a softer tone. "Tell me what happened."

Her lips opened as if to speak, but no sound emerged. Her freckles stood out in bold relief in a face so pale, it rivaled the wall behind her in whiteness. It was as if her hair had absorbed all the color from her skin and streamed like flame-colored silk to her shoulders.

"What's wrong?" he prodded.

"Look behind me," she managed to say.

Quentin glanced over her left shoulder. His eyes located the pile of mail, then zeroed in on the card. Since the letters were computer generated in large print, he could read the words from where he stood.

Leave, or next time it will be a rattler.

As before, the message was reinforced by a crude drawing. This time a snake coiled around the stick figure of a woman, the forked tongue poised a hairsbreadth from her face.

"Stay right here," Quentin ordered. Grasping the card by one corner, he flipped it over. Instinctively he reared back. God, how he hated snakes. Quickly he dropped his large handkerchief over the brilliant color photo of a rattlesnake.

In his years as a law officer he had learned that absolute innocence was alien to the human heart. Everybody had something dark they wanted to keep hidden, including him. His experiences had hardened him to the extent that nothing people did shocked him anymore, yet the maliciousness he perceived behind this harassment of Merrilee was greater and uglier than any he had encountered before. Crimes rooted in deep passion and erupting in moments of crisis were natural to the human condition and thus understandable, but this cold-blooded, calculated malice seemed to be rooted in pure evil.

Merrilee stood as still and as stiff as he'd left her. Compassion and protectiveness toward her surged through him, hardening his resolve to catch whoever was terrorizing her. For an instant he hoped that the miserable son of a gun would resist arrest. Grasping her lightly by her upper arms, he turned her to face him.

"Were you just leaving or just coming back?" he asked.

"What?"

"You're all dressed up. Were you just going out?"

She shook her head. "Coming back."

Standing this close to her in the strong afternoon light, he noticed that her skin was as fine-grained and smooth as his grandmother's heirloom Dresden china. He hoped that she was a hell of a lot tougher than that delicate porcelain. He took her hand, which was cold, far too cold for the relatively mild October day.

"We'll go into the house, and I'll fix you something hot and sweet to drink. My grandmother always said you needed something hot and sweet when you'd experienced a shock." Quentin opened the door with the key she'd left in the lock and led her to the kitchen. "Why don't you sit down while I see what I can find."

The first three cupboards he opened were empty. She either didn't cook or hadn't had a chance to go grocery shopping yet. In the fourth he found a small supply of staple goods, including four boxes of tea: English breakfast tea, Earl Grey, Darjeeling, and chamomile.

"Which tea do you want, Merrilee?" Quentin was conscious that this was the first time he'd addressed her by her first name. Would she notice? Would she mind?

"The Earl Grey."

Quentin busied himself with placing the kettle on

the stove, then setting out cups and saucers and the sugar bowl. He glanced at Merrilee from time to time, but she appeared oblivious to his activities, staring at the tabletop. He prepared the tea the way his grandmother had taught him, remembering all the times he'd shared this ritual with Gran during those first weeks he'd been back from Afghanistan. He hadn't slept worth a damn then. Being old, neither had she, so they ended up in the kitchen together at three o'clock in the morning. Looking back, he realized that those latenight talks with her had helped him more to come to terms with his experiences as a soldier than all the debriefings and therapy sessions with military personnel.

If only he'd stayed in the mountains then and not taken the job in the VA hospital in southern California. But he had felt obligated to try to help the men who'd been physically and emotionally hurt. Heading up the hospital's security force, he'd met Ellen, and with her had begun a whole new set of nightmares.

The ringing of the timer on the stove roused Quentin from his introspection. Removing the tea bags from the pot, he looked at Merrilee. Her color was better. He sat beside her, filled her cup, and added three teaspoons of sugar before he pushed the cup toward her.

Merrilee picked up the spoon. She stirred the tea and kept on stirring, her thoughts obviously on something else. Finally Quentin reached out and stopped her hand.

"Drink," he ordered.

She cradled the cup in both hands as if warming them before she took a sip.

Her fingernails were short and unpainted, which surprised him. Then he remembered seeing the music video of "Sundown" on television; she had accompanied herself on the guitar. That explained the shortness of her nails. Actually, there was nothing about Merrilee that hinted at her glamorous profession. She dressed conservatively, and the only makeup she wore that he could see was mascara on her lashes and a rose-pink gloss on her lips. She could easily blend in with all those upper middle-class women on their way to their PTA meetings or luncheons, though she was probably better-looking than most.

"Who could hate me that much?" she asked.

Her question caught him unprepared. "Maybe the motive isn't hate."

Merrilee looked at him, waiting for him to elaborate.

"It could be love, the flip side of of hate."

She shook her head. "I told you Hank Corian couldn't have anything to do with this."

"I didn't mean him. I was thinking of a love affair gone wrong since then."

"There hasn't been a love affair since then."

Unaccountably that pleased Quentin. He tried not to show it. "The second most common motive is money. Who is your beneficiary?"

"The state, I guess. I haven't made a will."

"Then we can rule out money. Could anyone benefit for some other reason from your . . . um, if anything happened to you? In your career, for example?"

"I don't see how. Maybe if I sang only one type of music and continuously stayed at the top of the charts, somebody might want to knock me off to get a chance at that spot, but I don't. Cumberland is a crossover band. That's probably what's held us back some. We sing pop, country, and even some blues."

"Why hasn't the band settled on one kind of music?"

"That's probably mostly my fault. I dislike doing the same thing over and over again. It's boring. Hap doesn't like it either."

"Hap's your lead guitarist, right? The one who wrecked his car?"

"Yes, for the fourth time, the dummy." Merrilee grimaced.

Quentin thought carefully before he phrased his next question. "Have you and Hap ever been more than fellow band members?"

"You mean lovers? No. It's stupid to get involved with someone you work with that intensely. I've seen several good groups break up over a romance gone sour. No, we're more like a family than anything else. That's why I'm so furious with Hap for his self-destructive behavior."

"Tell me about your real family. Where are they?"

"As far as I know, there's only my Aunt Hazel, my mother's sister. Would you believe that today's the first time I met her in my entire life? She's in the Maple Lane Nursing Home."

"How about your parents?"

"I don't remember either of them. My father was apparently unluckier than Hap. He wrapped his Chevy around an oak tree when I was three. My mother died a year later." Merrilee broke off. She stared into her teacup as if she could read her fate there. Musingly, she continued. "All these years I pictured my mother as a redhead. I thought that's where I got mine, but Aunt Hazel said Mom's hair wasn't red."

"Maybe you inherited it from your father."

"No. I saw his photo on the back cover of the one album his band made. His hair looked dark."

"Merrilee, don't you remember anything about your mother? You were four when she died. Most kids have a few memories of that age."

She shook her head, her expression unhappy. "No. I don't even recall anything of my first year in the orphanage and foster homes. My first memory is of my fifth birthday, and maybe I remember it only because I have a photo of me blowing out the candles on the cake."

"Don't you have any earlier pictures, anything of your mother's?"

"No. I guess everything was lost in the fire."

"Merrilee, how did your mother die?"

"In the fire that destroyed our cabin."

Quentin's scalp tightened, always the first sign that something wasn't right. "Where were you during this fire?"

She shrugged helplessly. "I don't know. When I was

older and asked that same question I was told that neighbors found me wandering in the woods near the blackened remains of our cabin, wearing only a nightie. Apparently I didn't speak a word for six days, and when I did, I couldn't remember anything other than my first name."

"Was your cabin near Browne's Station?"

"Yes. I begged and plagued Willadean until she took me there, but by then there wasn't much left. The cabin was in a small hollow off Laurel Mountain Road. About halfway up the mountain."

Very casually Quentin asked, "Do you remember the neighbors' names who found you?"

"Yes. They were listed in the report Willadean received when she became my guardian. They were Otis and Della Smith. But they don't live there anymore. At least they didn't when Willadean and I drove up the hollow. I was twelve then."

Quentin took a small notebook from his pocket. "What are your parents' names?"

"Reba Jones Ingram and Rafael Ingram." Merrilee watched him write the names into the book. Then, matching Quentin's casualness, she asked, "Why all these questions about my early life? Surely you can't think that anything that happened back then can have a bearing on my being harassed now?"

It was Quentin's turn to shrug. "Unless it's some weirdo who gets his kicks out of terrorizing celebrities, it has to be somebody connected to your personal life. You insist that it can't be anyone in your group or your former fiancé. You claim you have no enemies. That leaves something that happened when you lived here before. That's logical. You agree?"

"Yes. And I don't really know whether I have enemies or not. I don't think so, but how can I be sure? How can anyone?"

Merrilee looked at him as if she expected an answer. "Sometimes you can tell, but not always. I'll take your latest fan mail with me and see what I can find out. Lock up behind me. I'll call you."

They walked to the front door. Quentin picked up the handkerchief-covered card and handed Merrilee the rest of her mail. Their eyes met. For a split second his breath caught. He found it necessary to take a deep breath before he spoke.

"I'll be in touch. Try not to worry too much." Quentin wanted to add something more reassuring, something comforting, but for the life of him he couldn't think of a thing. Quickly he slid his aviator sunglasses on and left.

In the middle of the afternoon the police station was quiet. It was too late for the early-morning domestic violence calls and too early for the after-school street racing, the evening tavern brawls, and the late-night burglaries. Quentin found his secretary/dispatcher leafing through a copy of *People*. When she saw him, she shut the magazine and followed him.

"Well, did you see her again? What's she like?" Naomi Kincaid planted herself before her boss' desk and looked at him expectantly.

"Naomi, who are you talking about?"

The secretary rolled her expressive brown eyes. "Who do you think? Who's come to this dead burg and brought a little glamour? Merrilee Ingram, of course."

"I thought you said you knew her." Quentin flipped through the mail Naomi had put on his desk.

Naomi lifted her shoulders in an elaborate shrug. "I did. I knew her as well as any of us knew her back in high school. She was sort of a loner. Well, in all fairness, she did work a lot after school, but even during the day she didn't hang out with anybody in particular. What's wrong? Bob Lee said there were some problems over to Miss Willadean's old place."

"Miss Ingram is fine," he said.

"Fine? What does that mean? What does she look like? Bob Lee said she was real dishy, but then he said that about the new waitress at the Wagon Wheel too, and you've seen her. Makeup applied with a trowel and no chin to speak of." Naomi paused for a second before she repeated. "Well, is she?"

"Is she what?"

"Dishy?"

"Yes."

"Is Merrilee as slender as she looks on television?" Naomi asked, and she sucked in her stomach.

"She's got a good figure." Quentin couldn't believe he'd said that. Grateful for the mail on his desk, he bent over it and pretended to read it.

Naomi whipped out the compact she always carried in her skirt pocket and inspected her face. Her skin still looked great, but she did carry those extra ten pounds around her hips.

"What was Miss Ingram like in high school?" Quentin justified this question to himself on the grounds that her present problems might have their roots in her past.

"As I said, she was a loner. During lunch she'd always go to the music department for special tutoring from the choir teacher. I guess she always knew what she wanted, and she worked real hard to get it. That's why she made it bigger than any of the rest of us. We invited her to our tenth class reunion, but she was on tour and couldn't make it. She wrote a real nice note explaining her absence."

"What about boyfriends?"

"You got to be kidding! With Miss Willadean as her guardian? Fat chance. My folks knew the old battle-ax, and every time I felt they were being mean and unfair to me, I thought of Merrilee and felt better. Imagine living with a woman who wouldn't let you wear makeup. That was even worse than not being able to date. Especially for Merrilee. She's a true redhead, and if there's one thing redheads need worse than anybody, it's eye makeup. They look washed out without mascara and eyeliner."

"There are always cliques in high school. Did she belong to any?"

"No, but she could have. The real 'cool' people like Heather Cunningham were in choir with Merrilee and tried to get her to hang out with them. Maybe they sensed that she'd amount to something. As I said, she worked a lot, and when she didn't, she was taking music lessons or practicing the piano or the guitar or learning new songs."

"Do you know anything about her family?"

"No. I always assumed she was an orphan."

Quentin pulled a notepad toward him and wrote a couple of names on it. He tore the sheet off and handed it to Naomi. "See if you can find addresses on these people. They used to live in or near Browne's Station."

"Otis and Della Smith," Naomi read out loud. "Will do, chief." She pivoted smartly and left.

Quentin leaned back in his chair, swung his long legs off the floor to rest his feet on his scarred desk, and thought. Ten minutes later he'd decided on a course of action. On his way out the door, he told Naomi that he'd be at the courthouse, checking records.

After he'd located Merrilee's birth date, Quentin hurried to the *Evening Standard*'s office to search for the issue carrying the report of the fire. He was fairly certain that a fire in which a woman had died would receive front page coverage.

All back issues of the paper had been transferred to microfiche. Adding four years to her birth date, Quentin found the story on the front page.

The initial article said the fire started in two places. In the follow-up story two days later, the fire was described as being due to "unknown origins." That was pure bull. He reread both entries. Either sloppy reporting had resulted in mentioning two points of origin in the initial article and was forgotten in the follow-up, or someone had convinced the reporter to forget it. Whenever a fire started in two places, it could be safely assumed that the fire had been deliberately set.

The follow-up article quoted Deputy Sheriff Wiley Chapman as hypothesizing that the "little girl somehow managed to get out of the cabin in time," but that she was in a "state of shock" and couldn't remember a thing. Quentin studied Chapman's photo. He'd been considerably younger then, but the sour, mean-spirited look that characterized the sheriff of Browne County now had already been visible.

Quentin hadn't realized that Chapman had been around that long. No wonder he had something on everybody who was anybody in the county, which enabled him to be reelected like clockwork. Even if Quentin hadn't smelled something fishy in the story, the fact that Chapman had been involved in the investigation would have prompted him to take a closer look into the fire that killed Reba Ingram.

For good measure, Quentin looked at the back issues of the previous year. Rafe Ingram's fatal accident rated four paragraphs on page three. On his way home from a gig at a roadhouse in the next county, the guitar player had apparently lost control of his car on the winding road. Reading between the lines, Quentin was certain that alcohol had been a contributing factor.

What he needed next was a copy of the original investigation file. Even though on the surface his relationship with Chapman was amiable, privately Quentin detested the man. Whenever he could, he avoided dealing with Chapman. Quentin looked at his watch. With any luck the sheriff should have arrived at the Wagon Wheel Cafe for his supper.

From his office Quentin phoned Deputy Walker and told him what he needed. He signed a couple of reports Naomi had placed on his desk while he waited.

"I'm sorry this took so long," Ira apologized, "but I checked twice to be sure. There's no report in our computer of the fire or of Reba Ingram's death. Are you sure you got the date right?"

"Positive. I just looked it up in the *Evening Standard*."

"Dang. I can't explain why we don't have a report. Since it happened out in the county, we'd have been called."

"I don't understand it either."

"The only explanation I can come up with is that when we switched over to computers, the file got overlooked or got wiped out accidentally."

"What happened to the original files?"

"As far as I know, they were burned. I'm real sorry about this."

"It's not your fault, Ira. Thanks anyway." Quentin swiveled his chair to face the window. Was it an accident, or had someone deliberately destroyed the file? He had no proof, but instinct told him it hadn't been an accident.

Temporarily stymied about what to do next, Quentin told Naomi that he was going out for supper.

Quentin's house clung to the side of Blue Creek Mountain on the street that formed the boundary between Browne's Station and the county. He'd bought the house for its view. It looked out over the narrow valley below and onto Laurel Mountain opposite. Quentin stood still for a moment, contemplating the shadowy, blue-green mass that was Laurel Mountain. What had happened in that hollow that resulted in a young mother's fiery death and her small daughter's loss of memory?

The newspaper reporter could have made an honest mistake in reporting two points of origin. Cabin fires, as most rural folks knew, were started by all sorts of things. Its having been late October, Reba could have heated the cabin for the first time that season, and the fireplace or stove could have caused the fire. Or a faulty electrical outlet. Or a bunch of rags resting next to paint thinner or any other flammable liquid.

The insistent barking of his dog propelled Quentin into action. He had found the black dog when it had been almost fully grown, nearly starved, and obviously neglected. He had built a dog run in his backyard and christened the dog Charlie. Filled out nicely, the mixed-ancestry dog greeted him effusively.

Quentin spent ten minutes throwing the tennis ball for Charlie to retrieve before he fed him and then re-heated the pizza he'd picked up for his own supper.

While he ate, he wondered what Merrilee was going to do for her evening meal. From what he'd seen, there wasn't much food in her kitchen. Being as slender as she was, she probably didn't eat that much, but still he worried. What was it about her that roused his protective attitude? She certainly didn't seem helpless. On the contrary. She looked as if she was very much in charge of her life. Whatever was prompting his concern, he'd better watch it.

He was in serious danger of becoming personally involved with the woman. There was a definite attraction between them. He knew she'd sensed it too, though he could be mistaken about that. Yet Merrilee hadn't flinched or pulled away when he had touched her hand, her shoulders, her arm. On the other hand, she'd been upset and afraid and might not even have noticed. For all he knew, this attraction could be all on his part. In any event, it was totally unprofessional and unacceptable. He reminded himself of that several times on his way back to the office.

As soon as Quentin entered the police station, Bob Lee jumped out of his chair, a look of excitement on his face. "I've got a lead."

"Me too," Naomi said, waving a piece of paper.

Chapter Five

In the gathering twilight Quentin glanced at the crude map in his hand. The unpaved county road was little more than a rutted lane. He nearly missed the sign. Age and exposure to the weather had bleached the green letters on the slightly warped wooden shingle suspended from the low, sagging front porch.

"J.J. Upton, Herpetologist," he read aloud. "Must be the place." He got out of the car, reached for his .38 Special, which he'd placed on the passenger seat, and clipped it to his belt.

Looking around the junk-strewn front yard, he gave the inhabitants a few more seconds to prepare themselves for a visit by the law. Even if it hadn't been a mountain custom to wait before approaching a house, Quentin had learned from experience that it was prudent to do so. The barking of dogs grew louder.

The front door opened. The man said something over his shoulder, and the barking subsided.

Quentin stopped. "Evening. I'm Chief Garner from Browne's Station. I'd like a word with J. J. Upton."

"That'd be my dad. What you want him for?"

The man, middle-aged, stocky, wearing denim overalls and a red and black checked flannel shirt, was wary, but no more so than most people who found a cop on their front steps. "I'm told he knows snakes. I'd like to consult him professionally."

The man relaxed. "Dad's out back. Come with me. He'll be glad of the chance to discuss snakes."

Quentin followed him to the back porch.

J. J. Upton was a wiry old man wearing a fishing hat with several lures pinned on it. He was sitting in a huge rocking chair on the back porch. When the aged hound lying beside him started to get up, he put a gnarled hand on the dog's head to keep him quiet. His son performed the introduction.

"Don't mind me not gettin' up, but the rheumatism is botherin' my knees somethin' fierce today. Take a load off, Chief," he invited, pointing to a gray metal folding chair.

Quentin eyed the flimsy chair doubtfully before he lowered his tall body carefully onto it. "I'm told you're an expert on poisonous snakes, Mr. Upton."

"Yup. Handled snakes for fifty years until the rheumatism made me retire. What do you want to know about 'em?"

Briefly Quentin told him about the copperhead

suspended from Merrilee's porch ceiling. He ended with the question, "Who would be skillful enough to do that?"

"I can't give you names. I've been out of the business too long for that."

"Okay. How about the kind of person who could and would do that? I mean, what kind of man. I can't envision a woman handling a snake."

"That's where you're wrong, Chief. The best snake handlers I knew were women. As a matter of fact, my best customers for live snakes in the old days were churches, and it was women who bought the snakes, took care of them during the week, and carried them to and from the services."

Quentin was surprised into silence. He hadn't expected that. "Tell me about these religious sects."

J.J. reached under his floppy hat to scratch his head before he spoke. "Well, they were small, independent churches that didn't belong to mainstream religious groups. I can't tell you much about their beliefs, because I saw only part of a service once when I delivered a cottonmouth. It was real emotional, though. That preacher sure knew how to whip 'em up until they were cryin' and rolling on the floor and speaking in tongues and grabbing up snakes." He shook his head.

"I'll tell you one thing. There's nothing meaner than a picked up snake. As much as I've handled snakes, I'd no more mess with them unless I wore high boots and thick gloves up to my elbows than I'd try to fly by jumpin' off a cliff. Them snakes had probably been fed just before the meetin' to make 'em sluggish, but still."

"Didn't any of the faithful ever get bitten?"

"Sure did. Got mighty sick too. A couple of them even died, but that was their own fault."

"How's that, Mr. Upton?"

"According to their beliefs, they weren't worthy to live because their faith wasn't strong enough."

Quentin digested that for a bit. "Did you ever get bitten?"

"Yup. But as I said, I always wore protective clothing and I had antivenom medicine with me. Snakebite, at least from snakes found in these mountains, isn't usually fatal unless the snake hits a vein or artery or strikes a child."

"As far as you know, are there any religious sects like that still around who secretly and illegally use snakes in their worship?"

"I don't know. I hadn't had much call for live snakes for that purpose since it was outlawed by the government. The last group I heard of was over to Mt. Hebron."

"Mt. Hebron? That used to be a town in the eastern corner of the county, right?"

"Yup. They consolidated schools, and the town sort of died. Weren't much of a town to begin with," J.J. added. "Probably nothing left there but a couple, three buildings at the crossroads. You got to drive to the other side of Laurel Mountain to get to it. You mind if I get myself a refill?" he asked, gesturing to his empty glass and the Mason jar.

"No. Looks like good, healthy spring water."

"Nothin' wrong with your eyesight, Chief. This

here . . . medicinal water helps the rheumatism when nothin' else does."

While the old man poured a generous slug of the homemade "medicine" into his glass, Quentin asked, "Anybody else you can think of who could handle a snake expertly enough to hang it from a ceiling?"

"The guys who took over from me filling orders for zoos, but they wouldn't do that kind of thing. Besides, they live way over in the next county."

"How about people who collect venom from snakes?"

"Naw. They keep their snakes in cages and take good care of them. They wouldn't take a chance on getting one of them killed. It ain't as easy to catch snakes no more. Too many people around. Our snakes are shy by nature and steer clear of people. They ain't the aggressive kind. They strike only if you get 'em good and scared or mad."

"So, what you're telling me is to look for somebody who belonged or secretly still belongs to a religious sect, preferably a woman who handles their snakes."

"Yup. In my pa's time, there was a lot of 'em around. You got to remember that they thought snakebite wouldn't hurt 'em if they believed strong enough."

"Thank you, Mr. Upton. You've been a big help." Quentin stood up, ready to leave.

"Anytime you need to know anything about snakes, stop by. Be glad of the company."

On the way back to town, Quentin kept thinking about what he'd learned. It would be worth his while to drive to Mt. Hebron and talk to the remaining residents. He'd also visit Della and Otis Smith, whose address Naomi had found. Perhaps it would be better if he took Merrilee along on that visit. After all, they were her former neighbors. Quentin knew he was making excuses to see her again even as he made them.

Quentin picked up a carton of cold Mr. Pibb from the soft-drink cooler at Winn-Dixie before he drove home. He drank a can while he played with the dog. Then he went inside and took a shower, but not even the hot water relaxed him. He was too keyed up. It was only seven-thirty, still early enough to pay a visit to the Smiths. They didn't have a phone, according to Naomi, so this might be as good a time as any to catch them at home.

Impulsively he dialed Merrilee's number. After all, the Smiths used to be her neighbors. She was at home and eager to go with him. She asked for thirty minutes to get ready.

When he saw her, he admitted to himself that she would have been worth an hour's wait. She wore jeans that clung to her slender figure in just the right places and a beige cable pullover. As they walked to his car, she unfolded a long shawl the color of the spruce trees on Laurel Mountain.

"Allow me," Quentin said, and he helped her drape the shawl over her shoulders. His fingers grazed the material, which was soft and a pleasure to touch. "What's this called?"

"Pashmina."

"Are you going to be warm enough?" Quentin asked.

He'd put on his dark brown leather bomber jacket to ward off the cool evening air.

"I think so." When he opened the car door, she said, "I've always wanted to ride in a police car."

"With the lights flashing and the siren howling?"

Merrilee laughed. "Yes. How on earth did you guess?"

Her laughter was as clear and as lovely as the sound of a silver bell.

When he headed for the ritzy residential section of town, Merrilee looked at him. "The Smiths live in Orchard Heights now? From what I remember of my one visit to the hollow, their cabin was a two-room shack. Ours must have been just like it. Did they suddenly strike it rich?"

"No. We're just cutting through Orchard Heights. The Smiths live in a hollow five miles beyond the subdivision."

At the far edge of this subdivision a large house sat slightly apart from the others and on top of the hill. Its facade and the wide drive leading through the huge expanse of carefully tended lawns were lit like a Christmas tree.

"The Buford place," Quentin said.

Merrilee shuddered. "It's imposing and as ugly as sin."

Quentin laughed. "That's what happens when you have lots of money and no taste."

"Where did you grow up?"

"In Lexington. Even stayed there for college."

"Then what did you do?"

"Thought I'd give Uncle Sam a few years. He

promptly sent me to the Middle East. Only it wasn't as fascinating as *Scheherazade and the One Thousand and One Nights* tales."

Merrilee waited for Quentin to continue, but he didn't. After a while she said, "Hap saw action in the service too. I've always wondered if that's what's behind his drinking and his recklessness."

"Could be."

She studied Quentin's profile, but it gave her no clue to his feelings. "The action doesn't seem to have affected you adversely. At least not where it shows."

Merrilee watched Quentin take a hand off the steering wheel and run it through his short, straw-blond hair.

"Combat affects different guys differently. It's like two kids growing up in the same family, the same environment, and one turns to crime and the other doesn't. That surprises a lot of people. It shouldn't. Each person is unique, so each experience will be interpreted uniquely."

"What you're saying is that something could happen to both of us together tonight, and each of us would see it and feel it differently?"

"Yes."

Merrilee thought about that for a while. "You're right. That explains how differently Hap and I would sometimes evaluate a certain performance and the audience's response to it."

"It wouldn't surprise me if we interpreted the nonverbal behavior of the Smiths differently tonight," Quentin said. He had turned into a side road that climbed steeply and crookedly up the west side of Laurel Mountain. "Keep your eyes open for Wood Creek Road."

After a few minutes, Merrilee saw the sign. "Right there."

"Good. Now count the paths leading off this road. We want the fourth on the right."

They found the Smith trailer without difficulty. A wide porch, running the length of the one-bedroom trailer, had been added. The mercury-vapor lamp illuminated the porch enough to show a long table crowded with the kind of wood carvings sold alongside quilts, cider, and fireworks at roadside stands during the tourist season.

Several dogs announced their arrival. Quentin and Merrilee stood by the car, waiting.

The door of the trailer opened. With the bright light behind him, the short, hefty figure of the man standing there appeared even more squat. Slowly, leaning heavily on a walking stick, he stepped out onto the porch. A shadowy figure watched from behind the sheer curtains of the window beside the door.

Quentin identified himself.

"Come on up to the porch," Otis Smith said. When they stepped up on the wooden floor, he stared curiously at Merrilee. "Who's that with you, Chief?"

Before Quentin could introduce Merrilee, a high, thready wail erupted from the trailer.

"Come on out, Della," Otis called over his shoulder.

Della's skinny figure ran the few steps toward Merrilee, then stopped abruptly. Della stared into her face, turned, and ran to cower behind her husband, where she made indistinguishable, tiny noises.

"Della, what's the matter with you? You're acting like you're a brick shy of a full load."

Skittering out from behind Otis and clutching her hands to her sunken chest, Della mumbled something.

"What's that?" Otis demanded, clearly displeased.

"I said it's her. Reba's girl."

Otis leaned forward to peer into Merrilee's face. "Well, dog my cats! I think you're right, Della. Don't you recognize us, girl?"

"No. I'm afraid I still don't remember anything that happened that night. That's why we're here. I'm hoping you can tell me something."

Another half-stifled cry caused Quentin to look at Della closely. The expression on her deathly pale face was one of pure fear. Why would Merrilee's mere appearance frighten the woman so? Quentin found Della's reaction so intriguing that he continued to watch her.

"I don't know as we can tell you much," Otis said after he'd satisfactorily arranged his bulk in a rocking chair.

"I would appreciate anything you remember. When I was twelve, I persuaded my guardian to take me to Piney Creek Hollow to talk to you, but you had moved."

"Yeah, when I got my disability from the mine," Otis said, rubbing his stiff leg, "and Della here took a job cookin' for Miz Buford, we decided to move closer to town."

"The social worker's report stated that you found me

the morning after the fire. Is that right?" she asked Della.

"Mercy, yes. You wasn't wearin' nothin' but a cotton nightie. Not even slippers on your little feet. It's a wonder you didn't get the lung fever. I wrapped you in my shawl and hollered for Otis to come and carry you."

"Why were you looking for me?"

"We wasn't the only ones lookin'. A whole bunch of folks came at first light to look for you. You see, the firemen didn't find your body in the cabin's ashes. So we knew you had to be somewhere in the woods."

"Who called the firemen?" Quentin asked.

"I did. The dogs' barking like crazy woke us up. We didn't see nothin' at first, but when the wind shifted, we could smell smoke. We jumped into my truck and drove to Reba's. But it was too late to put out the fire. The whole cabin was in flames."

Otis stopped. Della forgot her nervousness and picked up the story. "Otis kicked in the front door. That's where we found Reba's body. He drug her clear, but before he could go back in, the roof collapsed."

"What about my mom? Did she say anything?"

"She wasn't breathing," Otis said. "I'm sorry."

"I stayed, and Otis drove to Miller's fillin' station down on the county road and called for an ambulance and to report the fire. We didn't have no phone. The ambulance and the fire truck came, but by then the cabin was a goner. When they didn't find your body, they organized a search party."

"And you found me?" Merrilee asked Della.

Della nodded. "Suddenly you was there. I don't know where you'd been, and you couldn't tell me. You couldn't say nothin'. I guess you was so bad scared, you plumb forgot how to talk."

"Did they ever find out what caused the fire?" Quentin's question was casual.

Otis paused for a moment before he answered. "Naw. My guess is, it was the stove. It was one of the first cold nights we had that year."

"Any idea how I got out of the cabin and my mother didn't?"

Otis shook his head. "Reba must have gotten you up and told you to run outside. She must have been closer to the stove, so the smoke overcame her."

"Did either of you see anyone drive past your house that night?" Quentin asked.

"No." Otis answered quickly and decisively.

"While your husband drove to the telephone, what did you do, Mrs. Smith?" Quentin asked, and he smiled at Della encouragingly.

"Well, I kept circling the cabin, tryin' to see if I could do something, but there was a solid wall of fire. After a while I walked back up the road and waited for Otis."

"Nobody drove past you?"

"No, except for that one car that pretty near ran me over."

Before Quentin or Merrilee could say anything, Otis spoke coldly to his wife. "Della, how many times do I have to tell you that you imagined that whole thing.

There wasn't no car." Turning to Quentin, Otis said, "I was coming back just then, and if there'd been a car, I'd have met it on the road. Della sometimes gets things mixed up. Don't you, Della?"

"Well, yes." Della wouldn't meet anyone's eyes. She rubbed her left arm in a soothing motion.

"Della, what color was my mama's hair?"

The question seemed to surprise Della, but she answered it readily. "Blond. Kind of like the color of wild honey. She was a real pretty woman, Reba was."

"Thank you. And my daddy? What color was his hair?"

"Dark brown. Almost black. Don't you remember nothin'?"

"I'm afraid not," Merrilee said.

"Neither do we. We've told you everything we know." Otis pulled himself up cumbersomely, signaling the end of the visit.

"I really appreciate your talking with me. Thank you. Good-bye." Merrilee smiled at Della and nodded to Otis. Quentin followed her off the porch after saying his good-byes. Neither of them spoke until they reached the county road.

"We'll have to catch Della alone. She wasn't telling us everything she knows," Quentin said.

"That's the impression I got too. Unless she really imagines things, as Otis claims."

"I don't think she's nearly as featherbrained as Otis makes her out to be."

"Then you think there could have been a car on the road that night?"

In her eagerness Merrilee laid a hand on his arm. Quentin felt a tingling sensation where she touched him. Several seconds elapsed before he answered her. "There could have been. Of course, she might not be able to describe it, and just knowing that there was a car wouldn't help us."

"Past our cabin there was nothing but a widening in the road for cars to turn around. So, if a car came from that direction, which Della says it did, the driver might have seen something, might know something about the fire."

Or have started it, Quentin added silently. "Yes, we definitely need to talk to Della alone." He paused for a beat. "Why the sudden interest in what color your mother's hair was?"

Merrilee shrugged. "You know how you form mental pictures of people you read about or hear about? I've always thought of my mother as having red hair like me."

"Sometimes red hair skips a generation. I've seen families where all the children had red hair except one, or only one out of the whole bunch was a redhead. Genes aren't all that predictable."

"I know."

On Oak Street Quentin walked Merrilee to her door and unlocked it for her. Handing her the key, he stood a mere foot away from her. Their eyes met and held.

"Thanks for taking me to see the Smiths."

"No problem. I enjoyed the company." Quentin noticed that her shawl had slid off her left shoulder. He reached out and gently pulled the soft material back up.

Merrilee murmured good night and walked into the house, closing the door softly behind her.

She hadn't objected to his touch, Quentin noted. With a smile he hurried to his car.

Inside, Merrilee stepped out of her black leather flats and watched Quentin leave from the window. Out of the corner of her eye she thought she glimpsed movement by the small rose garden on the side of the house. She watched for a while but saw nothing suspicious. She must have imagined the movement. She picked up her Gibson and worked on the melody of a new song for a while. But she wasn't in the mood for composing, so she went upstairs.

Something made her stop to gaze out the back window from which she saw her backyard and part of Peggy's. This time she definitely saw a dark figure slip behind the crepe myrtle bushes that marked the boundary line. Fear shot through her. What should she do? Quentin wouldn't be home yet for a while.

Merrilee ran to the phone and dialed Peggy's number. "Peggy, is Howard at home?"

"Sure is."

"He didn't go outside just now, did he?"

"Mercy, no. Why? What's wrong?"

"I saw somebody lurking out by the crepe myrtle bushes."

"I'll have Howard take a look."

Before Merrilee could protest, Peggy hung up. Howard wasn't a young man, and the intruder wasn't spying on him. She hadn't meant to put him in danger. She had no choice but to help him.

Merrilee took the gun from under the bed and rushed downstairs. Her hand shook as she very cautiously opened the back door and slipped silently into the night.

Chapter Six

At first Merrilee heard nothing but the pounding of her own heart. Keeping to the shadows as much as possible, she crept toward the stand of bushes separating the two properties. As she came closer, she heard a twig snap. Seconds later grunts and curses alerted her to a struggle taking place a few feet away.

"Howard? Howard, where are you?" Merrilee sprinted toward the bushes. A human form emerged and ran straight into her. Falling, she instinctively grabbed at the body. Her left hand connected. Cloth ripped. The figure cursed, freed himself roughly from her grasp, and hightailed it toward the front of the house. Merrilee picked herself up and turned toward the bushes.

"Howard? Are you okay?"

"Yeah. The son of a gun got away from me." Howard emerged, holding his chin.

At that moment Peggy burst through the back door

and raced toward them as fast as her short legs would carry her.

"Howard? Merrilee? Are you okay? What's going on?"

Peggy's flashlight illuminated Howard's bleeding lip. "Oh, my word. You're hurt."

"Come into the house," Merrilee urged.

"It's nothing," Howard protested valiantly. Flanked by the women, he trooped into Merrilee's kitchen. She placed her Colt on top of the refrigerator. Howard stuck his into the waistband of his pants.

"Let me look at your mouth," Merrilee said.

"It's nothing. I told you. The son of a gun got a punch in before I hit him. His lucky punch is the only reason he got away."

Both women tut-tutted over Howard's bloody lip.

Merrilee felt awful. "I'm sorry, Howard. I should have called the police right away, but I wanted to be sure it wasn't one of you out in the backyard for some reason. It didn't occur to me you'd rush out there like the cavalry."

"Well, the day I can't protect my property is the day they should haul me off to the burying ground."

"It's not too bad, hon," Peggy said. She moistened a paper towel at the sink and wiped away the blood. Merrilee wrapped a couple of ice cubes in a clean dish towel and told Howard to hold it against his lips to keep the swelling down.

"Quit fussing. The both of you," Howard said, though he looked as if he didn't mind all that much being fussed over.

Merrilee called the police station. The dispatcher promised them a patrol car within ten minutes.

True to the dispatcher's word, Patrolman Bob Lee arrived. From his back pocket he pulled a notebook that looked small in his huge hands. Before he could write down the particulars, Quentin's car braked to a screeching halt before Merrilee's house. He sent Bob Lee to check the neighborhood for a man on foot while he asked them to repeat the sequence of events.

"If you're sure you don't need a doctor, Howard, why don't you and Peggy go on home. There's nothing else you can do here," Quentin said. "Tomorrow morning I'll come to look around outside and see if I can find some good footprints. Would you mind walking around the front to your house? I don't want any possible evidence messed up out back."

Merrilee walked her friends to the front door and thanked them again. Then she turned to Quentin. "I'm sorry you had to come all the way back here. I seem to be causing you and your department no end of trouble."

"It's hardly your fault that somebody in this town is acting crazy."

"Then you think this is connected to the warnings and the snake?"

"Probably."

"Couldn't it have been a vagrant?"

"Possibly, though vagrants usually run."

"Oh, that reminds me," Merrilee said, taking the button out of her pocket. "When he ran into me, I reached out to keep from falling and tore this off his coat." She handed Quentin the button. "It's too big to be a shirt button. Looks to me like it came off a jacket or an over-coat."

"An overcoat, I'd say." Quentin pulled a small plastic bag from his pocket and placed the button inside.

"Are you really coming tomorrow to look for foot-prints? What good are footprints?"

"They're fairly accurate indicators of a person's height and weight."

Merrilee rubbed her forearm.

"Are you hurt? Let me see."

"It's nothing."

"I don't believe you."

"When I grabbed him, he shoved me. That's all."

Quentin took her hand. He pushed up her sleeve to look at her arm. He touched her skin where it was red. Merrilee liked the gentleness of his hand.

"This will turn black and blue. I'm sorry he hurt you."

For a second or two her mouth was too dry to speak. "I'll live," she finally managed to say. Merrilee smiled weakly when Quentin released her arm. As if by mutual consent, each took a step back.

Then Bob Lee's arrival ended the charged silence between them. The officer had found no one on foot.

"He probably had a car parked a couple of blocks away. We'll canvass the neighborhood tomorrow," Quentin said. "Maybe somebody saw something."

Merrilee suspected that this was a long shot but said nothing. As instructed once again by Quentin, she carefully locked up behind him and Bob Lee. She was halfway up the stairs when she remembered the gun on top of the refrigerator. She came back down to get it.

Voices in the backyard woke Merrilee the next morning mere minutes before her alarm clock was set to go off. Looking out the window, she saw two men bent over something in the rose bed. They must have found the footprint Quentin was hoping to find.

After a lengthy phone conversation with Gladys Vernon, Merrilee had learned that if she wanted to speak to her aunt's physician, she would have to catch him after his early-morning visit at Maple Lane.

She ran downstairs to start a pot of coffee before she took a quick shower and dressed.

Sipping her coffee, she waited until the last possible moment before leaving, hoping Quentin would come. He didn't. She was appalled at how disappointed she felt.

All the way to the nursing home she lectured herself on the folly of falling for a man at this point in her life. Some nutcase was threatening her, she was about to become acquainted with her only living relative, and she had at least seven more new songs to write—a daunting task by itself without all the other distractions around her, including Quentin. Especially Quentin.

Dr. Albright met her in the reception area of the retirement home. He reminded Merrilee a little of a television physician Willadean used to watch on one of the soaps.

"What would you like to know about your aunt?" Dr. Albright asked when they were seated in uncomfortable wing chairs.

"What's wrong with her? She isn't that old."

"No, she isn't," he agreed. "I suspect she never took care of herself. You know, good nutrition, proper rest, preventive checkups."

"Is there anything specifically the matter with her? When I came the other day, she was heavily sedated."

"Among other things, she doesn't sleep well."

"This was in the early afternoon. Should she have been drugged like that?"

"She's almost constantly in pain from severe arthritis. Mrs. Peterson also suffers from osteoporosis, and she has a bad heart."

Merrilee was silent for a moment. She hadn't expected such grim news. "Isn't there something you can do for her?"

"Beyond making her comfortable? No."

"Nothing? What about all those fancy operations and miracle drugs your profession is so proud of?"

Dr. Albright shook his head. "At her age the osteoporosis is irreversible, and the kind of heart problem your aunt has can't be fixed with an operation. I'm sorry, Miss Ingram."

"I'm sorry too. I didn't mean to jump all over you."

He smiled at her. "That's okay. Shows you care about your aunt. And I didn't mean to imply that it's hopeless. Once we stabilize her and with proper care, your aunt can lead a relatively pain-free, satisfying life."

"Really? You mean she might be able to leave here?"

"If we can build her strength up, she might."

Merrilee's thoughts were racing. Maybe she could add on a bedroom downstairs so Hazel wouldn't have to climb the steps. Yes, that was a possibility. But what would she do when she had to go on tour? Hire somebody. Maybe Peggy would be willing to look in on Hazel during the day, and she could hire a practical nurse to spend the night.

Almost as if he could read Merrilee's thoughts, Dr. Albright said, "Miss Ingram, I said maybe. Right now your aunt is very weak and run-down. She'll need special care for quite a while yet."

"I understand. Is there anything I can do?"

"There just might be. Your aunt hasn't been eating the past couple of days. See if you can get her to take some nourishment."

"I'll try."

"Good." Dr. Albright stood up. "I'd better get to my office, or we'll run behind all day long. Nice meeting you, Miss Ingram."

"I appreciate all you're doing for my aunt. Thank you, Dr. Albright."

Hazel was lying on her back, her eyes closed, the breakfast tray on the nightstand untouched. The hands lying on top of the blanket were so thin that Merrilee could see each vein clearly under the pale, paper-thin skin. She sat in the chair beside the bed.

"Aunt Hazel? You want some breakfast?"

Hazel's eyes flew open. "You *are* real. I thought maybe I dreamed you."

"I'm real. I'm Merrilee. Reba's daughter."

"I know. I've been praying hard to God to let me live long enough to meet you and to try to explain to you, to beg your forgiveness." She broke off, as if the few words had exhausted her.

"Please don't talk now." Merrilee looked at the breakfast tray. "Why don't I help you eat some of this food? Dr. Albright said we had to take good care of you so you could get your strength back and get out of this place."

She lifted the metal covers off the dishes on the tray. "Mmm. Looks like oatmeal with brown sugar and cinnamon on top. Toast, jam, and honey. Orange juice and tea. Not a bad breakfast. Now then. Can you sit up? "I'll—" Merrilee looked at Hazel, and the rest of her sentence died in her throat. Silent tears coursed down the lined, worn face. "Aunt Hazel, why are you crying? What's wrong?"

"Everything." Hazel sniffled.

Merrilee pulled a tissue from a box and handed it to her aunt. "Tell me about it."

"Your being nice to me makes it worse." A fresh flood of tears gushed from Hazel's eyes.

"Okay. If it'll make you feel better, I'll start fussing and yelling at you."

Hazel blinked the tears from her eyes. When she saw Merrilee's smile, she said, "You have a sense of humor just like Reba's."

"I don't remember my mother. Tell me about her," Merrilee suggested, "while you eat some of this breakfast." She cranked Hazel's bed up until she was in a sitting position. Then she placed the tray on the bed and poured a cup of tea. "I know you said she was a blond, but other than her hair color, do I look like her? Even a little?" Merrilee nudged the plate of toast toward her aunt, who took a piece.

"You sure do." Hazel nibbled on the toast while she studied her niece's face. "You got Reba's small, straight nose and her mouth. And that same shape to the face. Oval, not round like mine."

"And the eyes?"

"No. Your mama's were more gray, not true blue like yours." Hazel's eyes filled with tears again.

Merrilee placed the bowl of cereal before her to distract her. "Here. They say oatmeal is very healthy."

A small smile pulled at Hazel's bloodless lips. "Then I should be in the peak of health. That's what we were raised on. What little cash we got we had to spend on things we couldn't raise or make ourselves, so we never had dry, store-bought cereal. We weren't real poor, not poor like some of the people I saw in Third World countries. Mama always put in a big garden, and we had a lot of fruit trees and berry bushes. We all helped put up vegetables and fruit for wintertime. Pa raised hogs, and we always had a cow or two for milk. No, we lived pretty good, only I didn't know that until I went off with Mose."

Her aunt seemed lost in thought, but since she was eating the oatmeal, Merrilee remained quiet, not wanting to distract her. Hazel ate about half the cereal before she pushed the bowl away.

"It's no use," Hazel said. "I've got to get this off my chest. Merrilee, I'm sorry I didn't send for you when Reba died. If I could change just one thing in my life, that's what I'd do differently. You must believe me. As God is my witness, I'd send for you."

"Please don't cry." Merrilee, who rarely cried, found it almost unbearable to watch anyone else cry.

"I didn't know then. I didn't know they paid me too. I didn't know." Hazel lifted her hands toward Merrilee as if in supplication.

"Aunt Hazel, what didn't you know?"

"Mose, my husband, always said we didn't have any money. But he lied. He was a preacher, and he lied. The missionary board paid me a salary too, and he never told me. Just took the money and said we were too poor to send for you. His lies kept me from raising Reba's child. Oh, God, forgive me."

Hazel's heartbreaking cry tore at Merrilee. "It's okay, Aunt Hazel. I grew up just fine. It's okay. Really. Please calm down." Her soothing words seemed to have little effect on Hazel. Merrilee grew alarmed. "Aunt Hazel, it wasn't your fault."

"It was. I was ignorant, and that wasn't anybody's fault but mine. You being a modern woman, you don't understand what it was like for girls like your mama and me here in the mountains. I quit school in the tenth grade because Pa said there was no use in wasting time with books since I was going to get married anyway. It was better for me to help Mama at home and learn everything a wife and mother needed to know."

When Hazel stopped talking, Merrilee lifted the water glass to her lips. She took a sip before she continued.

"I was seventeen when I married Mose. Two years later we left for India. Until then the farthest I'd been away from home was Whitesburg. The first seventeen years of my life Pa told me what to do, and then Mose took over. I didn't make my own decisions except for what meals to cook until I became a widow. I was so green. I have no excuse for not fighting Mose about sending for you except that I was green and dumb. I was dumber than dammit. There, I've said it and cussed at the same time."

Ordinarily Hazel's small act of defiance would have been amusing, but there was so much pain connected with it that Merrilee's heart felt heavy. "Maybe we weren't meant to be together back then. Have you thought about that?"

"Yes. That's what I told myself. That if it was God's will, we'd get together someday."

"And now we have."

"Except you could have been with me all those years if Mose hadn't lied about the money."

"You can't live in the past, Aunt Hazel. It's over and done with. You must concentrate on getting your strength back."

Hazel drank the orange juice, which Merrilee lifted to her mouth. Then she leaned back against the pillows, obviously tired. Merrilee set the tray on the nightstand. "I'll leave now so you can get some rest."

Hazel's eyes flew open. She looked at Merrilee, her expression alarmed and fearful. "You will come back?"

"Of course, I will. And I'll see if we can get you a private room."

"Oh, no! You mustn't."

"Why not?" Thinking that Hazel was worried about money, Merrilee added, "I'll pay what your retirement check doesn't cover."

"It isn't that. I can't take up a whole room. It wouldn't be fair. I don't need it. The space I have here is just right."

"But you'd be so much more comfortable in a room by yourself. It won't be a hardship for me to pay. Truly."

"It isn't the money. I've got money. Don't you see? I would be taking up more than my share of space."

"Your share? I don't understand."

"If all living space on this earth were divided equally and fairly, this is about all I'd be entitled to," Hazel said, pointing to her corner of the room. "Because of my spinelessness and ignorance, I harmed you and some other people. I did what Mose said to do without questioning. Don't you see that I can't add any more wrongs to the ones I'm already guilty of? I'm just fine right here."

"Aunt Hazel—"

"No, no. Because of what we did, Mose and me, there's already been so much bad karma. I'm fine right here."

Seeing how agitated her memories made Hazel, Merrilee took her aunt's thin hand into hers and held it. "It's all right, Aunt Hazel. Don't get upset. I'll come and see you again tomorrow."

"Promise?"

"I promise." Merrilee stayed, holding her aunt's hand. Her mind was in a whirl. All these years she had bitterly resented Hazel, and all these years her aunt had been tormented by guilt. Merrilee tensed with anger each time she thought of Hazel's deceitful husband.

That reminded Merrilee of Hank. She had truly loved him. They had been happy until, flush with first success, he'd turned into a petty tyrant, forbidding her to continue her career. Suddenly he expected her to throw over years of hard work to live only for him. Perhaps she would have tried to do that, but, fortunately, she was spared that humiliating experience. She had caught him in bed with one of the backup singers from the recording studio.

The next day Hank claimed he'd been drinking and didn't know what he'd been doing. Luckily Merrilee had been blessed with one of those flashes of insight that seemed to strike her from time to time. She had realized that if she stayed with Hank, her life would be one long series of his drunken infidelities. Shrugging, she dismissed thoughts of Hank.

The shallow, even breathing told her that Hazel was asleep. Merrilee pulled the blanket up to her aunt's chin. Touching her frail arm, she thought Hazel's skin seemed cold. She glanced around the room until she located the thermostat. With determined steps she approached it. Unfortunately, the knob designed to adjust it had been removed. She rapped her knuckles against the gauge.

"Won't do no good," the woman in the other bed said in a stage whisper.

"It won't?"

"Naw."

"Have you tried it, Mrs. . . . ?"

"Lovell. Ethel Mae Lovell. And I've tried everything. Jiggling it, hitting it with a slipper, even talking to it."

Merrilee picked up a washcloth from the basin by the door. "Do you mind if I use some of your ice water?"

Ethel Mae shook her head. She watched intently as Merrilee walked back to the wash basin, poured some of the icy water over the cloth, wrung out the excess, and covered the thermostat with it. "Is that going to work?"

"It should."

"I hope so. We keep telling that Vernon woman that us old folks got thin blood and need extra heat, but she don't believe it. Of course, she's always hot, which ain't surprising, since she's got as many extra layers on her as a fatt'nin' hog."

"I'll speak to her about the heat," Merrilee promised, noting that Ethel Mae didn't look very hopeful.

Gladys wasn't in the recreation area or in the lobby. "Mrs. Vernon? Where are you? Is anybody here?"

Merrilee called in the general direction of the offices behind the lobby.

"We already tried. Nobody seems to be home."

Merrilee froze. That voice. If she lived to be a hundred, she wouldn't forget it. Every Sunday and Wednesday evening for eight years she'd had to listen to it, sitting perfectly still in that hard pew for an endless hour. By turns cajoling, threatening, and pleading, it relentlessly promised hellfire and damnation unless everybody did the will of the Almighty as interpreted by Brother John. As she grew older, it was the interpretations that bothered her.

Merrilee's stomach ached the way it used to. The half-repressed fears came crashing into her consciousness. Then she remembered that he had no power over her. Not anymore. Not since Willadean died and freed her of the necessity of going to Brother John Cosgrove's church. Merrilee took a deep breath before she turned around.

A gasp escaped from the woman with him. Sister Bridie, even smaller and thinner and more colorless than Merrilee remembered her, stood her habitual two steps behind her husband. She'd clapped a work-worn hand over her mouth. The washed-out blue eyes looked at Merrilee with something akin to horror.

"Well, we heard you were back, Sister Merrilee," John said.

"Don't call me sister. I'm not a member of your congregation."

"Yes, you made that perfectly clear."

His eyes, those awful pale eyes that could blaze with the light of fanaticism, surveyed her shamelessly. Merrilee felt revulsion rise in her like bile.

Bridie took a small step forward and shook a pointed finger at Merrilee. "Willadean wasn't even cold in her grave yet before you defied her most cherished wish and stopped coming to church. God'll get you for that!" After this brief outburst, Bridie stepped back.

"Maybe so, Mrs. Cosgrove, but don't worry about it."

"It's never too late to return to the fold," John said.

"I already belong to a church," Merrilee started to explain, but one look at his face told her that he still thought his and only his church was the chosen one. There was no point in arguing with him. "If you'll excuse me—"

"Why are you here?" Bridie demanded.

"In Browne's Station or in the nursing home?"

"Both."

Though John remained silent, Merrilee could see he was keenly interested in her answer. Why?

"Your aunt promised us already, so don't you go changing her mind!" Bridie yelled. Her voice was shrill and edged with a trace of hysteria.

"Hush your mouth, Bridie," John commanded.

"You two stay away from my aunt. She's too ill to be hounded by the likes of you." Merrilee glowered at Bridie, who lowered her eyes, though her mouth was pressed into a stubborn, relentless line. It wasn't nearly as easy to cow John. He looked coolly at Merrilee. A small, cruel smile curved his mouth.

"Sister Hazel's a member of our sister church in India. We're here to minister to her spiritual welfare."

Merrilee forced herself to calm down and to speak civilly. This wasn't the time or the place for a confrontation with Brother John. "I appreciate your concern, and I'm sure you can remember Hazel in your prayers at your church. You don't have to do it here. Her doctor ordered rest and quiet. Right now she's sleeping." Merrilee crossed her arms, assuming an unmistakably defensive, protective posture.

"That's all right," John said, stopping whatever his wife was going to say. "We'll come back some other time to visit with Sister Hazel. Come, wife."

"Please phone first to check if she's up to having visitors." Brother John managed to incline his short-cropped graying head in a civil manner, but the look he shot Merrilee was anything but friendly. She knew that even though she'd won this skirmish, they were far from beaten. They'd be back. If they upset Hazel in any way, Merrilee swore she would get a court order, if necessary, to keep them away.

At the lookout point high on Laurel Mountain, the man was once again seated behind the wheel of the Lincoln. This time his co-conspirator didn't make him wait.

"What's the problem now?" the sheriff asked without so much as a hello.

"The chief of police is sniffing around our songbird. I'm worried. Does he suspect something?"

"There's nothing to suspect."

"Then why is he hanging around her?"

The sheriff sighed. "According to my informant, Quentin is a single, healthy, normal male. She's an attractive, unmarried woman. Surely even you can figure out what that means." There was contempt in his voice.

"You think that's all that's going on?"

"Yeah. Just nature taking its course. Don't call me unless you really got a problem. Everything's under control. Trust me." The official car pulled away.

"Trust me," the man in the Lincoln mimicked. He'd trust him when hell froze over. It was time he himself took a hand and set a few things into motion.

Chapter Seven

Merrilee straightened up, then held the rake with one gloved hand while pressing the other against the small of her back. Raking leaves was more strenuous than she had remembered.

"Slow down. You don't have to rake the entire cemetery by yourself."

Merrilee smiled and turned in the direction of the pleasant masculine voice. "I was beginning to think you'd only show up for the food, not the work."

Quentin shook his head at her with mock severity. "Shame on you for thinking that the chief of police would set such a bad example. I even brought my own trash bags." He pulled one out of the package and shook it open. "Here. You hold it, and I'll scoop the leaves in."

"Okay. But after a while we'll trade off. Scooping is harder than holding."

"My hands are bigger. It'll go faster if I scoop." Quentin slipped on a pair of brown work gloves. "The quicker we get done, the sooner we can eat. I passed the tables where the ladies are setting up the food and was sorely tempted to stop. It smelled so good."

Quentin scooped, pushed, and shoved handfuls of leaves into the bag Merrilee held for him.

Merrilee glanced over the town's oldest and biggest cemetery, marveling at the number of people busily raking the leaves from the oak, ash, and sweet gum trees that surrounded the graveyard. The large turnout was even more surprising since this was Wednesday, a weekday. Originally the cleanup had been scheduled for the coming Saturday, but the weather forecast promised a cold front moving in, so Mrs. Buford, the head of the committee, had rescheduled it.

Quentin wore jeans, a University of Kentucky Wildcats sweatshirt, and sneakers. This was the first time Merrilee had seen him out of uniform. He looked good, she thought—more than good—in jeans. Lean and sexy with enough firm angles to rival a Springsteen album cover. A melody line popped into her head. She spun it out. It would work just fine.

"Merrilee? Hey, Merrilee?"

Roused from her musical musings, she looked up at Quentin. "What?"

"The bag's full."

Her eyes focused on the bulging plastic bag. "Oh." She smiled a little sheepishly and pulled the top shut.

"Well, well. Isn't this nice? Glad to see the chief of police working so hard."

Merrilee raised her eyes. They stopped on the sheriff's star pinned to a gray uniform. Her heart skipped a beat in anxiety before she remembered that she wasn't on tour and the sheriff's presence didn't mean automatic harassment of the band. Quentin straightened up.

"Sheriff Chapman, have you met Miss Ingram?"

Quentin performed the introduction. Merrilee didn't offer her hand, guessing that the sheriff wasn't into shaking hands with women. He raised two fingers to touch his hat but didn't take it off.

"Are you enjoying your stay in Browne's Station?" he asked. His smile revealed nicotine-stained teeth, but his flat, mud-colored eyes belied the smile.

"Yes, thank you."

"Are you planning to be with us for a while?"

"Yes, I am. My aunt is a patient in the Maple Lane Nursing Home." Merrilee could have kicked herself for justifying and explaining anything to the sheriff. It was a conditioned response, the result of too many encounters with unfriendly deputies in the early years when the band played just about every honky-tonk and club from Maryland to west Texas.

"Well, I hope your aunt gets to feeling better soon," Chapman said.

"Thank you, Sheriff." While Chapman said goodbye to Quentin, Merrilee watched the sheriff carefully. Chapman didn't fit the beer-bellied, redneck, small-town southern sheriff image so often presented by Hollywood. Everything about Chapman was thin: his body, his ginger-colored hair and mustache, his smile. And probably his compassion and empathy as well. Not a man to antagonize. She shivered.

"What's the matter?" Quentin asked. "I have a Windbreaker in the car if you're cold. Want me to get it for you?"

Merrilee shook her head. "No, thanks. I'm not cold." Continuing to watch the sheriff as he headed toward the food table, she said, "That man gives me the creeps. He's got that mean and hungry look."

"Chapman won't win any popularity contest, that's for sure."

"But he gets reelected?"

"Yes."

"How?"

"It's nothing as crude as stuffing ballot boxes. He's been a lawman in the county for a long time. Thirty years or more. Chapman's observant, sly, crafty, and smart. I know he likes to pose as kind and mild-mannered, except he's anything but."

"He's become a fixture, and the county's stuck with him."

"I guess we could be stuck with somebody worse."

"We ran into worse types all over the place."

"We?"

"The band. They would take one look at the guys' long hair, and I knew exactly what would follow. We learned to keep an attorney on retainer who made local contacts and could get us legal help quickly. I despise lawmen like Chapman."

"I'm not crazy about him myself."

Merrilee turned toward Quentin. "But you have to work with him."

"Yes. That's why I have to treat him with a measure of courtesy. My jurisdiction ends at the city limits. There are times when I need his cooperation. I wonder what he's doing here." Then Quentin shrugged, dismissing the sheriff.

Very casually Merrilee asked, "Any news on the evidence?"

"Nothing on the button yet. The net came from fish netting that's sold in every minnow and bait shop in the country. We're still checking on the card."

"We may never find out who sent me the lovely messages."

"We will. There's no such thing as a perfect crime. Actually, most criminals are fairly stupid. Sooner or later the person harassing you will make a mistake."

"I wish it were sooner rather than later."

"I know," Quentin said softly.

Somebody rang a bell, announcing that the food was ready. Since they'd been working at the far end of the cemetery, they were among the last in line to get food. Peggy was one of the ladies behind the serving table.

"I laid a tablecloth for you right over yonder." She pointed. "The flower-sprigged one. Now, be sure you take some of my chicken and my pies." She raised a hand up to her face to shield it from the other woman working farther down the serving line. In a stage whisper she instructed, "Take the slaw in the green glass bowl. That's Loretta's. She makes the best slaw in these parts."

"When can you join us?" Merrilee asked.

"Since y'all are the last in line, I'll be with you directly."

Merrilee pointed out Peggy's pies. Not shy, Quentin took a piece of the sweet potato pie as well as the cherry and apple.

When he saw Merrilee's amused expression, he said, "Hey, I don't get this kind of food very often. I aim to take advantage of it."

"Where do you usually eat?"

"Here and there. I'm a fair cook, but I don't often have time to fix a decent meal. And I don't know how to make pies. Maybe Peggy could teach me."

Merrilee stared at him.

"What?"

"I don't meet a man every day who is sure enough of his masculinity to risk being caught baking a pie."

Quentin shot her a long, level look. "You have any questions about my masculinity?"

She felt her face redden. "No."

"Good. This is hardly the place for me to prove it to you, had it been necessary."

"Maybe I've been around show business types too long," she murmured, knowing her cheeks were still pink. "Is cooking your hobby?"

"No. It's a necessity. I like to eat, but the food has to

be good. In Browne's Station that means you have to learn to cook, unless you're happy alternating fried chicken and barbecued ribs with fast food."

"And you like greater variety?"

"Yes. California spoiled me."

Merrilee led the way to the cloth Peggy had laid out for them. They lowered themselves to the ground. "What took you to California?"

"A job. I headed up the security in a VA hospital shortly after my last tour of duty was over."

"You didn't like California?"

"It was okay."

"Then what brought you back to Kentucky?"

"A couple of things." Quentin paused, staring into his ice tea glass. A few seconds later he said, his face expressionless, "My wife died."

"I'm sorry." Both were silent. Merrilee wished she could think of something appropriate to say.

Quentin looked at her. "It was a long time ago. Sometimes I think maybe I only dreamed that part of my life. It seems so unreal now."

"You said a couple of things brought you back. What was the other?"

"This," Quentin said, pointing to the mountains surrounding the narrow valley in which Browne's Station nestled. "Didn't you miss these mountains when you were gone?"

"I haven't been back to Browne's Station, but I've toured Kentucky, Tennessee, and the adjacent states many times. Now that you mention it, I've always enjoyed coming back to this area. Willadean used to call this God's country." They concentrated on their food, but all the while Merrilee wondered how she could ask him about his late wife without seeming overly nosy, insensitive, or too interested in him.

"Why don't you just ask me?"

"What?" Merrilee looked at Quentin. "How did you know I wanted to ask you something?"

"Sometimes I know exactly how you feel, what you think. That's strange. At least for me it is, because this has never happened to me before with anyone else."

That admission stunned her. Men, at least the ones she'd known, didn't usually disclose their feelings so honestly. All her adult life she'd yearned for a man who could and would. Had she found one? It was almost too good to be true. The silence lengthened between them, filled with anticipation.

"You were wondering about my wife." When he saw Merrilee's expression, he added, "I was curious about your ex-fiancé, so I assumed you'd want to know about my wife."

She nodded.

"I met Ellen at the VA hospital. She was a nurse there, very capable, very caring. I admired her dedication and compassion. I didn't realize until it was too late how much her dedication and compassion cost her. She got hooked on pills. Pills to help her fall asleep, pills to help her get going in the morning, pills to keep her weight down, and heaven only knows what else she took them for."

Merrilee waited for him to continue.

"I didn't know how many she was taking. It didn't

occur to me that she had a problem. Maybe because she was a nurse, or maybe she just hid her addiction very well. One day she took the wrong combination. I was on duty at the hospital. A nurse who came by the apartment to pick her up for work found her. It was too late. She died. Alone."

Quentin spoke without expression. It was almost as if he were reciting something that had happened to someone else. It took a moment before she realized that this was the only way he could talk about his wife. Merrilee reached for his hand and intertwined her fingers with his. She pressed his fingers. When he returned the pressure, she knew it was all right for her to speak.

"Quentin, it wasn't your fault. I've watched a musician friend try to get her husband off drugs. She can't, no matter how hard she tries. He has to do it himself. Even if you had known about Ellen's pill problem, you couldn't have helped her. Nobody could but Ellen herself."

"Objectively I know that, but I still feel . . ." He trailed off and shrugged.

"Guilty?"

He nodded.

Merrilee thought about Aunt Hazel. Guilt was a heavy burden. "Quentin, one of these days you'll have to forgive yourself."

"You're the only one here I've told this." He looked at her with eyes that mirrored his surprise, his wonder, and his apprehension.

"I won't tell anyone."

"I know. You're a woman who keeps her own counsel."

"A bit of a loner?"

"It takes one to know one, as the old adage says."

"It's not necessarily a bad thing to be alone. After a performance, it's absolutely necessary for me to be alone so that I can regroup and recoup my energy." She studied Quentin. "I imagine in your line of work you see things that make you want to stay away from people for a while."

Quentin nodded but did not elaborate.

They ate in silence until Peggy joined them.

"I got held up," she announced. She was carrying a plate of food in one hand, a napkin and a plastic fork in the other.

Quentin jumped up and held her food while she lowered herself to the ground.

"Thank you kindly." She smiled at Quentin's gallantry.

"What held you up?" Merrilee asked.

"A couple of your favorite people arrived late. They picked up their plates. Then they saw Mrs. Buford and her family. Since they're the kind that toadies up to the rich and powerful, they naturally had to go and say hey. Then they couldn't make up their minds as to what kind of pie to take."

"Who was it?" Merrilee asked.

"Brother John Cosgrove and his wife."

"My all-time favorite couple in the world."

Peggy wrinkled her forehead. "Willadean was a down-to-earth, sensible woman except where them two

were concerned. I never understood why she thought so
highly of them."

"Maybe she liked Brother John's preaching,"
Quentin offered.

"She must have. I went to church with her a couple
of times but wasn't impressed. I don't go in for all that
shoutin' and hollerin'. All that was missing were some
snakes to turn it into one of those old-fashioned back-
woods meetings."

"Snakes?" Merrilee asked, and she looked at
Quentin. "Peggy, what do you know about snakes being used in churches?" She leaned forward expectantly.

"Not much. My ma used to tell of a church she went
to once when she was young where they brought in
poisonous snakes for the service. Liked to scared her
to death."

"Where was this?" Quentin asked.

"Let me see." Peggy stared at the chicken wing in
her hand as if it were a map. "Must have been over to
Mt. Hebron. Yeah, that's where it had to be. I could
ask her when I see her at the nursing home. That is,
if it's one of her better days, when she remembers
things."

"I'd appreciate it. And if she could remember the
names of some of the people who handled the snakes,
it would be even more helpful," Quentin said.

"Does this have something to do with the snake on
Merrilee's porch?"

Quentin nodded.

"Well, I'll be! I'll ask Ma the first chance I get. To

think a churchgoing person would do something like that."

"Peggy, have you run into Brother John at the nursing home when you visited your mother?" Merrilee asked.

"Yeah. I'm pretty sure I saw him come out of your aunt's room a time or two. Why?"

"Maybe I'm wrong, but I don't think it's good for her to have him visit. She isn't supposed to get upset or excited. He told me he's been there to pray with her, and, well, I know his style of praying. It's not exactly comforting. I'm going to ask Dr. Albright about banning the visits."

"Brother John ain't gonna like it if he's kept from visiting one of his flock or someone he hopes to add to it. You watch out for him, girl," Peggy warned.

"If you have to ask him to stop his visits, give me a call. I'll be there to lend you moral support," Quentin offered.

"Thanks. I might take you up on that." They both knew his presence would do more than add mere moral support. Merrilee tried to remember the last time someone had stood up with her to face an unpleasant situation. She couldn't. This would be a novel and welcome experience. She smiled warmly at him. A little surprised, he returned the smile. Then he scooped up the last crumbs of his third piece of pie.

"Peggy, this was the best pie I've ever eaten. I couldn't tell you which was better. You're one excellent cook." Quentin sighed hugely, appreciatively.

"Well, thank you." Peggy blushed at the praise like

a young girl. Merrilee was pleased that Quentin had been generous with his compliments.

"There's coffee at the side table," Peggy told them.

"I'd love a cup," Merrilee said.

"Me too. How about you, Peggy?" he asked.

"No, thanks. I can't drink but the one cup in the morning, but you two go ahead. I need to go and say hey to some folks over yonder."

They deposited their paper plates in a big trash barrel. Merrilee had noticed a sort of informal head table behind which a very large woman held court. Mrs. Buford, she presumed.

"Hey, Chief. Who's that with you?"

The voice hailing Quentin was high, childlike. Merrilee looked around for a ten-year-old.

"Come on over here."

Shocked, Merrilee realized the voice belonged to Mrs. Buford.

"We've been summoned," Quentin murmured in a low aside.

Using the same low tone of voice, Merrilee asked, "Who does she think she is, the queen mother?"

"More like the queen herself."

As they approached the physically commanding presence, the other people drifted away as if dismissed. Mrs. Buford wore a tentlike, pink and white flowered dress that had obviously been bought in an exclusive shop but which fitted her badly. It revealed the lines of one of those uncompromising girdles that made one scream for heaven's mercy. Her eyes looked like two small black craters in a full-moon face.

Quentin introduced Merrilee to Mrs. Buford, who regarded her with unflinching eyes. Her small mouth pursed, as if she didn't approve of what she saw. She lowered herself carefully into a sturdy wooden chair, which creaked in protest.

"It's not often we get a celebrity in Browne's Station. Maybe you can help us out with some of our civic projects," Mrs. Buford fluted.

Merrilee couldn't decide what she resented more: being called a celebrity in that supercilious tone or being recruited as slave labor by the local queen bee.

"I'm afraid I have very little free time. I'm not on vacation." Merrilee softened her words with a brief smile.

Lurlene waved a bejeweled hand dismissively. "Fiddlesticks. You have free time if you make it. We need everybody's help with restoring the Watkins House and turning it into a historic site. My daughter, Petulia, will call you and let you know how you can help. She's in charge of the project."

Merrilee had been unaware of the younger woman hovering nearby. She was as thin as her mother was fat. Looking more closely, Merrilee could see a family resemblance. Petulia had the same small, close-set black eyes and dark brown hair as her mother.

"Petulia's married to Earl Mainwright, our lieutenant governor, who is running for the United States Senate. You must have noticed the posters?" Lurlene said, bristling with pride.

Merrilee hadn't made the connection between the charismatic lieutenant governor and the wealthy local family. What she'd heard of the man had impressed her. She couldn't hold his in-laws against him. "I've seen the posters."

"My husband's the best choice for the senate seat, no matter what some people might say." Petulia's voice was vehement, even though nobody had said anything about her husband.

Merrilee looked at her speculatively, wondering why the woman seemed so nervous and so hostile. Petulia lit a cigarette. When she looked up, Merrilee involuntarily took a step back. The look in the woman's eyes could only be described as hate-filled.

"We'd better get back to the leaves." Quentin took Merrilee's arm in a protective manner.

"Nice meeting you," Merrilee said, lying politely, for Lurlene regarded her with the same hard-eyed resentment as her daughter. When they were out of earshot, Merrilee asked, "What do you suppose those two women hold against me?"

"I don't know, unless it's the resentment of two plain women toward a beautiful one."

"That's ridiculous. I'm not beautiful."

Quentin's hold on her elbow forced her to stop. He looked at her face. She wasn't angling for a compliment. "You really don't think you're beautiful? Who made you think you're not?"

"I have eyes, for heaven's sake. They tell me that I'm as freckled as a guinea hen, and my hair is wavy and as red as . . . It's not strawberry blond or Titian or auburn but red-red."

The sun, which had been playing hide-and-seek with

the clouds all day, broke through, igniting Merrilee's hair. Quentin looked at it with admiration. "It sure is red. There's no denying that, but I think it's a beautiful color. Come on, Merrilee, who convinced you that you weren't beautiful?"

"Willadean, I guess. But she always added that it was a blessing if a woman wasn't beautiful. It would keep her from tempting men and so save her from succumbing to the sins of the flesh. She was big on denouncing sins of the flesh."

"That was her misguided way of protecting you."

Merrilee shrugged. "Whatever her reasons were for telling me red hair and freckles were homely, it's immaterial. I'm convinced that my looks have nothing to do with the resentment of those two women. What could it be?"

"It doesn't matter. Neither of them is exactly known for a sweet disposition or a charitable heart. Come on." Quentin led her to the far edge of the cemetery where they had worked before.

After a while they ran out of trash bags. While Quentin went to fetch some, Merrilee took the opportunity to lean on her rake and look around. The man and the woman working nearby stopped. Something about their frozen postures caused Merrilee to look more closely. A moment later the woman started to scream. Dropping her rake, Merrilee ran toward her.

Chapter Eight

Merrilee didn't know how long she stood there staring at the man's face or, rather, what was left of it. Watching big black ants emerge from the matted hair and crawl purposefully down the blood-covered, smashed features, she desperately wanted to look away, but she couldn't.

Suddenly the earth seemed to tilt beneath her, and for a horrifying second she thought she would pitch forward onto the grisly body. A pair of strong hands grabbed her shoulders to steady her.

"What's wrong? Are—" Quentin's voice broke off as he looked over her shoulder. "Sweet Jesus," he muttered. Hesitating only a split second, he spun her around to face him. Merrilee's skin was as white as the collar of the blouse she wore under her blue sweater. He thought she might be on the verge of losing consciousness.

"Take a deep breath," he ordered. "Again. Once more. Good. I want you to look at that old oak tree up there." Quentin pointed at the tree. When she did, he added, "I want you to count the main branches. When you're finished, count them again. Block out everything else but the tree. Concentrate."

Merrilee nodded, her eyes dutifully fastened on the tree.

"I'm going to let go of you, and you'll be fine." He released her shoulders but stayed close, ready to catch her should she fall. When she remained upright, he turned toward the man and the woman who were clinging to each other on the other side of the shallow grave. The woman's screams had subsided into frantic sobs.

Quentin addressed the man. "Mr. . . . ?"

"Jarvis. Pete Jarvis."

"Mr. Jarvis, I have to use the radio in my squad car. I don't think anyone will come to this part of the cemetery, but if they do, will you tell them to stay back? I want to keep the crime scene as uncontaminated as possible. I'll take the women with me."

"Sure thing, Chief."

Quentin escorted the women toward the area where they had eaten lunch. Merrilee was pale, Mrs. Jarvis red-eyed. Both were quiet. He motioned to Peggy to join them.

Peggy frowned when she saw their somber expressions.

"Peggy, will you stay with Merrilee and Mrs. Jarvis? They'll fill you in on what happened, but keep what they say under your hat. I don't want to start a stampede to the old part of the cemetery."

"Okay."

"I'll be back as soon as I radio for backup." Turning to Merrilee, he asked, "Will you be all right?"

"Yes," she said, her voice faint.

His expression softened briefly. "If anyone asks why they can't go back there, make up some story. We don't want a panic on our hands."

As soon as Quentin hurried off, Peggy wanted to know what had happened. Merrilee told her.

"Oh, my stars! You poor lambs," she said to both women. "How awful for you. No wonder you look all done in. Let's sit over here under the tree." Peggy led the way to the tree, and the women sat down. "What's this world coming to? I remember when the worst crime around here was making moonshine, stealing a chicken from a farm, or the occasional Saturday night fight at the roadhouse. Now we got threatening letters, snakes on people's porches, and murder."

Merrilee saw Quentin walk back toward the old cemetery. A few minutes later he returned. He'd put on his reflector sunglasses. He paused to check on the women.

"Do you know who the dead man is?" Merrilee asked him.

"No. We can't look for any identification he might have on him until after we photograph the scene."

"He hasn't been under those leaves long, has he?" Merrilee asked.

"No. The autopsy will give us a better idea of the time of death."

"The killer didn't do a very good job of hiding the body."

"Maybe he didn't have much time. It isn't as easy to dispose of a dead body without being seen as the movies make it appear. And maybe this was supposed to be only a temporary hiding place." Quentin paused, thinking. "You know, ordinarily hiding a body in this part of the cemetery would be a pretty good idea. Most of the graves are so old, there are no family members left to visit them. The killer probably didn't know that the graveyard cleaning had been moved up to Wednesday."

"Or maybe it didn't matter if the body was discovered today," Merrilee added.

"That could be true too, especially if the killer has come up with an alibi, or if he thinks there's no chance that we'll connect him to the body." Quentin glanced at his watch.

"A couple of deputies should be here very shortly. They'll set up a barricade over there to keep everybody back. As soon as the ambulance and the coroner arrive, everyone working in this cemetery will know something's wrong. I don't want you ladies to say anything to anyone. Okay?"

The women agreed readily.

"I'll make an official statement to the press later."

"I've been thinking about your comment that this old part of the cemetery is a good place to hide a body," Merrilee said, "and it occurred to me that a stranger wouldn't know that the graveyard extends back into this small hollow. You can't see it from the road. So, wouldn't the murderer have to be somebody who's very familiar with Browne's Station?"

Quentin nodded. "And the victim has to be a man somebody around here would recognize."

"Is that why the face was smashed in?"

"Likely that, or extreme rage."

"Mercy me," Peggy whispered. "I've lived here for years. If you want me to, I'll take a look at him."

"I hate to put you through that experience."

"Well, Merrilee survived it. I reckon I can too."

"Thanks. I appreciate that. We'll do it after the coroner gets through with the body."

Two deputies arrived, loaded down with photographic equipment and wooden barricades. Quentin showed them where he wanted to set up. While one deputy stood guard at the barricade, the other went with Quentin to photograph the body. By the time the ambulance and the coroner arrived, the cemetery cleanup work had come to a standstill. People crowded right up to the barricade, jostling one another to get in front, even though they couldn't see much from there either.

"It sure is taking them a long time," Peggy said.

"If you've changed your mind about trying to identify the body, I'm sure Quentin will understand."

"No. It's okay. I said I'd do it. Here they come now."

The ambulance attendants carried the stretcher. When they reached the women, they stopped.

"Are you sure you want to go through with this?" Quentin asked.

Peggy nodded.

Quentin unzipped the body bag to reveal the victim's face.

Merrilee braced herself before she looked. She concentrated on the man's hair, which was graying. She guessed him to be in his late fifties, maybe early sixties.

Peggy studied him. She shook her head. "I've never seen this man before. I'm pretty sure he doesn't live in Browne's Station."

"Merrilee?"

"I don't think I've seen him either. Sorry."

"Thanks anyway." Quentin closed the body bag and motioned the attendants to go on. "Peggy, can you drive home on your own? I want Merrilee to come to the station with me."

"Sure thing."

Quentin escorted the women through the crowd, ignoring the questions fired at him. All he said was, "I'll have a statement in time for the six o'clock news."

They helped gather up Peggy's pie plates and her dishes and carried them to her car. Quentin made certain she drove out of the cemetery without being mobbed by the crowd.

Quentin walked Merrilee to the squad car in silence. He started the car and drove toward headquarters. She studied his profile. The dark glasses hid his eyes, but the furrows in his forehead suggested that he was deep in thought. Merrilee kept quiet as long as she could. Finally she burst out with, "Are you going to make me wait till the six o'clock news too?"

Quentin turned his head, startled. "What?"

"Are you going to tell me why you're taking me to the station, or is that a state secret?"

"I'm sorry. I was trying to figure out something."

"About the dead man?"

"Yes. There was no identification on him."

"Maybe it was a robbery that went wrong. The mugger hit him harder than he meant to."

"Could be, except the labels have been torn out of his raincoat, his pullover, and his shirt. I've never heard of a mugger doing that."

Merrilee stared at Quentin. "If the killer went to so much trouble to keep his victim's identity a secret, then our theory that he didn't care if we found the corpse has to be wrong. Which means he's someone who didn't know the date for the cleanup was moved up, or he didn't have a chance to find a different hiding place."

"That leaves a lot of the residents of Browne's Station as suspects."

"If the killer thinks the victim's clothes could help identify him, then they must be distinctive."

"The clothes are the reason I'm taking you to the station."

Since they were almost at their destination, Merrilee restrained her curiosity. Quentin pulled the car into his reserved spot.

Inside the flat-roofed brick building an elderly man sat behind the dispatch radio unit.

Quentin introduced her to Mace and then asked, "Where's Naomi?"

"She had a dental appointment. Boy, is she going to be miffed she's missing all the excitement." From his gleeful expression it was obvious Mace was happy he wasn't missing it.

"As you can see, murder isn't an everyday occurrence around here," Quentin remarked dryly.

"Chief, Buddy Odom from the *Evening Standard* called twice. You want to talk to him when he calls back?"

"No. I'll have a statement ready later. We'll be in the lab." Quentin took Merrilee's arm and led her past a couple of glassed-in cubicles and an office with his name on the door to a larger room that reminded her of her high school science class. The deputy who'd helped Quentin take the pictures pointed to a plastic bag before he disappeared into the adjoining darkroom. The red lightbulb above its door blinked, warning everyone to stay out.

Quentin pulled on a pair of surgical gloves. He took the victim's coat from a bag and spread it out on the table. "Merrilee, please look at it but don't touch it. What can you tell me about this raincoat?"

"It's called a Burberry. People who pay this much for a raincoat refer to it by that name. The reason I know this is because Hap dated our yuppie accountant for a while. She gave him a Burberry for his birthday." Merrilee noted the severed thread where the tag had been ripped out. She looked at the buttons and gasped. "Did you see these buttons? And one of them is missing!"

He nodded, his face impassive. "Tell me what you think."

Merrilee had to swallow before she could speak. "These buttons look like the one I tore off the guy who hit Howard."

"That's what I thought too."

"Do you still have the button, so we can compare them?"

"No, I sent it off for analysis, but we have a photo of it." Quentin opened a drawer. From a manila envelope he removed a picture, which showed a close-up of the button.

"That's it! That's the missing button."

"A perfect match." Quentin stared thoughtfully at the coat.

"This doesn't make any sense. Intruders who creep around in someone's backyard don't usually get themselves murdered, do they?"

"Not usually. Not unless this one saw something he wasn't supposed to see, or if he wasn't an intruder to begin with."

"But if he wasn't, what was he doing, spying on me?"

"I don't know. Yet." Quentin tore off the gloves with more force than necessary and dropped them into a trash can.

"I don't know him, so it's unlikely that he has a reason for harassing me into leaving town."

"When we find out who he is, we'll start getting some answers."

"You think you'll discover his identity?"

"Most likely, but it'll take time."

"If he was the one harassing me, there won't be any more threats, will there?" Merrilee saw the doubt in Quentin's eyes and grew pale.

"I'm sorry," he said. "I wish I could tell you that it's all over, but I can't."

"This is like a bad dream, only a nightmare stops when you wake up, and this doesn't."

The despair in her voice knifed through Quentin. He reached for her and held her, silently comforting her. He hadn't planned to embrace her, at least not in the police lab while investigating a murder in which she might be peripherally involved. It wasn't professional, but it felt so right. His arms tightened around Merrilee. She wasn't crying. He almost wished she were. Tears might release some of the tension he felt as he held her. He stroked her hair. After a moment he felt her relax a little. That small sign of trust elicited a rush of warmth to Quentin's heart.

The sudden crackling of the overhead intercom jerked them apart.

"Chief, Channel Five is here, and so is Buddy Odom. They won't leave without speaking to you."

Quentin swore silently. "I'll be right there." The buzzing noise stopped as Mace switched off the intercom. "Merrilee, you stay here. I'll send someone to take you home."

His protective gesture didn't escape her. She knew he could get a lot of publicity for himself by taking her out front to face the media. Deep gratitude swept through her, threatening to bring tears to her eyes. The "thank you" she managed came out in a hoarse whisper.

Quentin acknowledged her thanks with a nod before he hurried from the room.

A few minutes later the deputy who had guarded the barricade came to drive her home.

The house was silent, and though Merrilee ordinarily welcomed the quiet, after the day's events she found it eerie and unnerving. Trying to calm her jangled nerves, she executed a series of diaphragmatic breathing exercises, took a hot soak in her deep, old-fashioned tub, and fixed herself a pot of herb tea. For once, none of these usually effective calming remedies worked. She still felt as tense as a guitar string.

Merrilee would have sought refuge in Peggy's warm, food-fragrant kitchen as she had many times in the past, but the Farmers were out visiting some member of their extended family.

Glancing at her watch, she realized that if she hurried, she could make it to the nursing home before visiting hours were over. Thanks to habit born of living out of a suitcase, all of Merrilee's clothes hung in coordinated outfits in the closet, enabling her to dress in a matter of minutes. She reached the nursing home in record time.

Gladys Vernon was talking on the telephone when Merrilee breezed past the front desk. The assistant administrator motioned for her to come to the desk, but Merrilee pointed to the clock and mouthed, "Later."

From the door of her aunt's room she could see that

the curtain had been drawn around Hazel's bed. Alarm shot through Merrilee. Ethel Mae, who was watching a rerun of the *Andy Griffith Show,* used the remote control to flick off the set the moment she saw Merrilee.

"Your aunt's probably asleep already. They had to give her a sedative earlier."

"Why?"

"She was powerful ashy."

Merrilee hadn't heard that expression in years. It took her a moment before she recalled what it meant. "Why was my aunt so upset?"

"That I don't know. I was out to the recreation room after supper," Ethel Mae said. "My guess is that it was them two Bible-thumpers. Their preachin' of hellfire is enough to make a person feel sicker than she already is."

"Are you saying that Brother John and Sister Bridie were here and upset my aunt?"

Ethel Mae nodded. "Stayed a good long spell too. I kept track, because I wasn't about to come back while they was still here."

"They won't be back if I can help it."

"Good. I don't cotton to them two."

Merrilee walked to her aunt's bed. Hazel's eyes fluttered open as soon as Merrilee took one fragile hand and squeezed it gently. "How are you, Aunt Hazel?"

"Drowsy," she murmured.

"I know. They gave you a sedative. Did Brother John and Sister Bridie upset you?"

Hazel murmured something, but the only word Merrilee thought she understood was *yes.*

"What did they want?"

Again Hazel's lips tried to shape words. Clearly frustrated, she tried again. This time one word came out clearly. "Money."

"They wanted money from you?" Outrage temporarily froze Merrilee's power of speech. Those two leeches wanted to extract money from an old woman in a nursing home! Though appalled, Merrilee believed them to be quite capable of something that crass and heartless. She remembered how successful Brother John used to be in eliciting donations from his gullible flock, including the usually sensible and levelheaded Willadean.

Merrilee patted her aunt's hand. "Don't worry about money. I told you I had enough to help you out. And don't worry about Brother John and his wife. They won't bother you again. I promise you that. Now, don't fight falling asleep. I'll stay a while, and I'll be back tomorrow. Sweet dreams." Merrilee bent down and kissed her aunt's lean cheek.

She kept her promise and sat with her aunt until Hazel's breathing was deep and even. Then she tiptoed around the bed. Ethel Mae looked at her expectantly.

"Is she asleep?"

"Yes. Ethel Mae, you seem to be able to get around pretty well. If I leave you some quarters, will you call me from the pay phone in the recreation room in case either John or Bridie Cosgrove try to visit my aunt again?"

"Sure. That is, God willin' and the creek don't rise."

Merrilee wrote her phone number on a piece of paper and handed it and several quarters to Ethel Mae, who dropped them into a porcelain jar marked DEN-TURES.

"Nobody thinks to look in this jar, but don't worry. I keep my teeth in the bathroom medicine cabinet at night," she confided with a sly wink.

"Good thinking. I really appreciate your help."

"Happy to do it. Gives me somethin' to look forward to."

Gladys Vernon sat behind the front desk. She rose when Merrilee approached. "Please sit down, Miss Ingram."

Merrilee wasn't even seated before Gladys launched into a defensive explanation.

"We had to sedate your aunt because she was terribly upset. And that, in turn, brought on an attack of angina pain. We had to calm her down in a hurry. We had no choice. Those are her doctor's orders."

"I understand. Thank you for helping my aunt." She saw some of the wariness drain out of Gladys. "What I want to know is, what upset her in the first place?"

Gladys shrugged. "I can only guess."

"Please do."

"She had visitors. Preacher Cosgrove and his wife."

Merrilee thought that Gladys was watching her closely to gauge her reaction. "I know them," Merrilee said, "but I'm not a member of their congregation, and neither is my aunt."

"That's good to know." Gladys appeared relieved.

"Generally we encourage visits by preachers because it seems to comfort our patients. Besides, some of them have no family left, so the church people are their only visitors. In your aunt's case . . ." Gladys' voice trailed off.

She was obviously waiting for Merrilee's reaction. "In my aunt's case she would be better off without those visits. As a matter of fact, I don't want the Cosgroves in her room again. What do I have to do to make sure that they won't bother her again?"

"Just get your aunt's consent. We'll keep them away from her."

Gladys pushed up the sleeves of her uniform as if she were ready to bodily prevent their visit. Merrilee thought she looked as if she almost hoped the Cosgroves would be foolish enough to try to push past her formidable physique to get into Hazel's room.

"I'll talk to Dr. Albright. Between the two of us I'm sure we can convince my aunt not to see them again."

This seemed to meet with Gladys' approval. Her long neck bobbed a couple of times as she nodded. "Dr. Albright will be back from his vacation in two days. As soon as you give me the word, the Cosgroves will be banned from the premises."

Merrilee suspected that Brother John and Sister Bridie must have irritated Gladys in some other matter. Upsetting Hazel alone wouldn't have been sufficient reason for the unflappable assistant manager to go on the warpath.

On her way home, she stopped at the Winn-Dixie

for groceries. She put them away before she remembered that she hadn't checked the day's mail.

There had been no hate letter in two days. If her tormentor followed the established pattern, she was about due for another message.

Using a scarf, she reached into the box and removed the contents. Merrilee spread the letters on the piano. The only one that looked suspicious was a nine-by-twelve padded manila envelope. She stared at it, her heart pounding. Briefly she was tempted to phone Quentin, but common sense took over. He was busy trying to solve a murder case. He had no time to come and help open her mail. Besides, more than likely it contained a cassette. Songwriters were always sending her cassettes of songs, hoping Merrilee would add them to her repertoire.

She squared her shoulders and picked up the envelope. She slit it open and shook the contents onto the piano bench.

"What on earth?" she muttered, looking curiously at the strange object. It wasn't until she read the message on the accompanying sheet of paper that she realized what it was. With a shudder of revulsion she fled from the room.

Chapter Nine

"**R**ight off I wouldn't have known what this was either," Quentin said, sliding the rattles off the piano top into an envelope.

The movement caused a faint buzzing noise, and even though it was probably only a pale imitation of the real warning sound rattlesnakes made before they struck, it caused Merrilee to break out in goose bumps. "Whoever is doing this must be sick."

"I agree. The question is, who knows you're afraid of snakes? I don't mean a little bit afraid the way most people are, but really, deeply frightened of them."

"I'm not so awfully afraid now, but when I was small, I was truly terrified. Even a photo of a snake would make me scream with fear."

"Merrilee, why do snakes frighten you so?"

Unhappily she shook her head. "As far as I know, I've never been bitten by a snake, so it's a completely irrational fear. I assume it's connected with the night of the fire and being alone in the woods."

"Who would know about your fear?"

Merrilee shrugged. "People who knew us, I guess. But who in heaven's name would remember that over twenty years ago a little girl was frightened of snakes? It's so trivial."

"You'd be amazed how often the seemingly trivial is the source of something major. The Farmers were close to you from the beginning of your life with Willadean. They would know of your terror of snakes."

"Now, wait a minute! There's no way either Peggy or Howard would do this to me. You're way off base."

"Take it easy." Her blue eyes blazed at him. In anger, Merrilee's red hair seemed to take on an even redder sheen. He lifted a hand in a conciliatory gesture. "I'm only doing my job, which is to suspect everybody automatically. Personally I don't consider the Farmers serious suspects, but, Merrilee, somebody in this town is doing this to you. Haven't you been able to think of anyone who might be holding a grudge?"

"No."

Quentin thought about the fire that had killed Reba Ingram. He'd have to keep digging some more as soon as he had a chance. And the religious sect handling snakes in Mt. Hebron. With the discovery of the body that afternoon, everything else had been put on hold. He had hoped that Merrilee's nemesis would take a little time off between threatening notes, but no such luck.

"Have you eaten supper?"

Merrilee shook her head. "I just got back from the nursing home."

"Then you sit down in the kitchen and rest. I'll cook. Come." Quentin took her hand and led her to the kitchen. "I hope you went to the grocery store since the last time I was here."

"I did."

"Good." Quentin opened the refrigerator door and bent over to study its contents at length. Somewhat puzzled, he asked, "Don't you ever eat anything besides salads and fruits?"

"Sure. I make pretty good sandwiches."

"Sandwiches? Don't you fix hot meals?"

"No. I don't know how to cook." When Quentin looked at her with a disbelieving expression, she added defensively, "Don't say that all women know how to cook. It's not a skill we're born with, and I never learned how."

He didn't say anything but continued to gaze at her with a faintly puzzled look.

Merrilee felt she had to expand her explanation. "When I lived here with Willadean, she always insisted that I practice my music right after school. Then, while I did my homework, she cooked supper. Later I had after-school jobs. When I left here, I spent my spare time practicing with bands and going to auditions. Then I started touring and recording, and I've never had a chance to learn to cook."

"Hey, it's okay. As far as I know, it isn't carved in stone anywhere that women must know how to cook," he said. "I've met women who didn't cook well, including my wife, but never one who didn't cook at all. So I was surprised. I wasn't being critical or judgmental. Okay?"

"Okay." Quentin smiled at Merrilee, a smile that soothed her and assured her that in his eyes it was truly all right if she was less than perfect.

"What you need, what we both need after a day like today, is comfort food. I know just the place where we can get it."

"Is it a fancy place? Do I need to change clothes?"

He thought she looked lovely in her dress of muted blues and greens. "Actually, you might be a little over-dressed. You may want to change into jeans and a sweat-shirt for maximum comfort. Or you can come the way you are."

"Where are you taking me?"

"To my house." Quentin watched her expression carefully. He was relieved when she didn't look as if she suspected him of ulterior motives.

"I don't want to put you to any trouble. We could get something frozen at the store and pop it into the oven."

"No way. Not tonight. We need comfort food."

"What do you consider comfort food?"

"Something hot and satisfying like pasta, mashed potatoes and gravy, a thick, rich stew with biscuits, French fries, gooey pies—stuff like that. Sound good?"

"Yes. Absolutely perfect."

"What do you consider comfort food? What do you do to relax?" he asked.

"The guys in the band invariably head for the nearest bar or buy a few six-packs, while I sit and strum my guitar and . . ."

"And what?"

Merrilee shook her head. "It's too juvenile and embarrassing."

"Come on, tell. I confessed to pigging out on food that's generally considered bad for you and that would earn me a stern lecture from every doctor in the country. Fess up."

"Promise you won't laugh?"

"I won't laugh." Quentin crossed his heart.

"I drink a big cola and practically inhale a couple of Moon Pies." Merrilee watched his face anxiously for any sign of his laughing at her. She saw his jaw all but drop to his chest.

"You mean those big, teeth-melting, chocolate-covered, marshmallow-filled disks sold all over the South that kids love?" Quentin couldn't stop himself from grinning.

"You promised not to laugh!"

"I'm not laughing. Just smiling. It's refreshing to find out that someone famous like you indulges in such an innocent vice." His eyes regarded her with amusement but also with warmth and affection.

"Swear you won't tell anybody I'm addicted to Moon Pies."

"Whom would I tell?" He was making an effort not to grin.

"I don't know, but those gossip rags displayed at

checkout counters all over the country would have a field day with this. I can see the headlines. *Popular Singer Subject to Sugar Binges. Merrilee Ingram Confined to Betty Ford Clinic to Kick Sugar Habit!* Or something more insidious," Merrilee said jestingly, but there was a serious undertone in her voice. "They can take one simple fact and twist it and embellish it with enough innuendo to turn a normal person into a fiend."

"I give you my solemn oath not to reveal your shameful secret."

Quentin looked anything but solemn. His light green eyes sparkled with amusement. Merrilee had never seen him so lighthearted. It made him look years younger and quite approachable, even wearing the khaki uniform into which he'd changed sometime since the graveyard cleaning.

"What are you thinking?" he asked.

Quentin had caught her staring at him. Averting her glance quickly, she said, "If you don't mind, I won't change clothes. It's getting late, and I'm hungry. Aren't you?"

"Very."

Meeting his eyes, Merrilee's heart thumped mightily. She suspected he was referring to a different kind of hunger, and even though that hunger gnawed at her too, it would have to remain unsated. Her life was in too much turmoil already to risk adding the emotional upheaval a romance brought with it. As if he'd sensed her thoughts, Quentin's expression lost its intensity.

"I only suggested changing into something less fancy because my dog has a tendency to get carried away when I have visitors. I'll try to restrain him."

Fifteen minutes later Merrilee witnessed Charlie's enthusiasm firsthand. The huge black dog launched himself at Quentin with a force that would have staggered a smaller man.

Grasping him firmly by the collar, Quentin held Charlie while Merrilee stroked his shaggy head.

"Please excuse his lack of manners. I acquired him when he was full grown, and I haven't been home enough to retrain him."

"How did you acquire him?"

"It was more a matter of his acquiring me. He showed up here last spring, limping and dragging his tail like a worn-out broom, his right ear half chewed off, his ribs sticking out so far, you could have hung your hat on them, so I fed and doctored him, and he's been here ever since. I know he's not much to look at, but I've grown to like him."

Merrilee felt a great rush of affection flood through her for this man who so clearly loved the dog who was uglier than homemade sin.

"Did you ever have a pet?" Quentin asked.

"No. When I was little I wanted one desperately, but Willadean grew up in the country, where you kept animals strictly for work purposes. You know, dogs guarded and hunted, cats kept the mouse population down, so she couldn't see any sense in keeping a pet.

As soon as I cut down on touring or stop altogether, I'm going to adopt a whole bunch of pets from an animal shelter."

"What'll you do when you stop performing?"

"Compose. When I first started out, I really loved performing, but now more and more I find myself wanting to stay put in one place and write songs, compose the score for a movie, and maybe even try my hand at creating a whole musical."

"Have you set a timetable for that yet?"

"No. I have some commitments through next summer. We're scheduled into the studio to cut a record in early spring, and we've signed to perform at a number of state fairs and music festivals."

Merrilee continued to pet the dog while Quentin refilled Charlie's water dish and measured out his ration of dry dog food. While the dog ate, she looked out over the valley. Lights were beginning to appear in Browne's Station below, which was shrouded in deep blue and purple shadows.

"You should see the sun come up over Laurel Mountain. It's truly spectacular. Actually, the reason I bought this house was because of the view."

"I can believe that."

"Let's go in before you get chilled," Quentin suggested.

Merrilee looked around the fifties-style kitchen with undisguised curiosity. "I can't believe how neat everything is. There isn't a single dish in the sink or on the drain board."

Quentin looked up from the sink where he was washing his hands. "I hate clutter. You waste too much time looking through it for what you need. I find it easier to clean up as I go."

"I wasn't being critical. I spend large amounts of my life in cramped quarters on the tour bus, where being tidy is necessary for survival. It makes me appreciate neatness."

While he dried his hands on a paper towel, Quentin said, "If you want to freshen up, the bathroom is the first door to your right down the hall."

The bathroom was as clean and uncluttered as the kitchen. Briefly, good manners struggled with her compelling curiosity about Quentin before the curiosity won out. Merrilee opened the medicine cabinet. The contents were sparse and neatly aligned. The top shelf contained a shaving mug with soap, a brush, and a safety razor. Merrilee had never seen a man use such old-fashioned implements. With a fingertip she touched the brush. It was baby soft.

She pictured him lathering the soap over his lean cheeks and jaw. He would be bare to the waist, she suspected, maybe wearing pajama bottoms or a towel draped around him. Quickly she washed her hands before her imagination could take her farther. She returned to the kitchen.

A half smile graced Quentin's face even before he looked up at her. He was washing a green pepper. "Would you like something to drink? A glass of wine? A can of Mr. Pibb?"

"A Mr. Pibb would be nice."

Quentin fetched two cans from the refrigerator and handed one to her.

"You don't have to feel obligated to drink something soft," she said, "just because that's all I drink."

"I like the stuff." As if to demonstrate, Quentin pulled the tab on the can and downed a good portion of it. "Don't you ever drink anything stronger?"

Merrilee shook her head. "I always felt that I needed to stay clean and sober in case I had to drive the bus or rescue the guys from the trouble they get themselves into. Besides, I've seen what alcohol and drugs can do to people. I don't want any part of it." Merrilee studied the top of her can.

"I've often wondered if my father had been drinking the night his car hit that tree. Sometimes I think he probably had been, and I get angry. If he'd been sober, he'd probably be alive today. My mother might not have been killed in that fire, and everything would have been different."

Quentin reached out and raised her chin with his hand. His voice was soft and gentle when he spoke. "Hey, you don't have to justify your disapproval of substance abuse to me. I've seen my share of the disasters it causes."

"I'll bet you have. For a moment I forgot what you do for a living. You don't drink either?"

"Rarely. Since I'm on call twenty-four hours, I can't afford to drink, even if I wanted to." With a wickedly sharp-looking knife Quentin chopped a peeled onion with deft, sure motions. He scraped it into the pan on the stove. "I used to smoke, but when I realized how it winded me when I ran, I quit. I figured it was dumb to let a suspect get away because I had foolishly damaged my heart and lungs by smoking."

Merrilee watched him chop the green pepper with the same skill and add it to the pan. "Speaking of suspects, any news on the body we found? I only asked because of the other threat that arrived in the mail. He could have mailed it before he was killed."

"Possibly." Quentin added the peppers to the pan before he continued. "We'll know more as soon as the autopsy is done."

"But you think someone else could have mailed the threat?"

Quentin nodded. Though she tried to hide it, Merrilee looked disappointed. He knew she longed to hear that the dead man had been the perpetrator, because that would mean the harassment would stop.

Reading his face correctly, Merrilee said, "Nobody can accuse you of sugar-coating anything."

"Lying or misleading you would only increase the danger to you. If you thought the person harassing you were dead, you'd stop being careful and leave yourself wide open to attack. I'd hate like the devil to see any harm come to you."

"Would you?"

"You'd better believe it."

Though his words were simple, the intensity with which Quentin uttered them belied their simplicity. If she allowed herself, she could easily believe them. A part of her longed to believe him with a fervency that dismayed her. It was the part of herself that had been hurt and rejected in the past when it reached out for warmth and love. The experience had taught her to be on guard against exposing that vulnerable side again.

"Why do you find it so difficult to believe that I care about you?"

Astonished, she met his gaze.

"It's written all over your face."

Merrilee didn't want to discuss this now. She wasn't even sure she could verbalize the reasons for her belief, but she guessed Quentin would insist on an answer. Taking a deep breath, she spoke.

"People claim to care about one another all the time, yet they hurt each other with frightening regularity. Words are cheap. They don't mean anything. You're a cop. How can you believe that people care or mean what they say?"

Quentin handed her a wooden spoon. "Please stir the vegetables.

Merrilee did.

Standing next to her at the stove, Quentin dropped handfuls of fettuccine into the boiling water in a tall pot. He turned slightly toward her when he spoke. "What you said is true. On one side there's a lot of indifference, a lot of hurt, a lot of wounded people who'd like to care but can't. But there's also the flip side to that, which balances things out. I believe there's a duality in nature. You know, like light and dark. Good and evil. Man and woman. Yin and yang. Life and death."

Quentin paused to shake salt into the boiling water. "As for my being a cop?" He shrugged. "It's true, I see a lot of the dark side of life. If I didn't believe in this duality, in the goodness and love that's on the opposite side of cruelty and hate, I probably would have to change careers and sell insurance or write advertisements or become a hermit on top of Laurel Mountain."

Merrilee watched him turn to the chopping block on the counter, where he placed a clove of garlic under the wide blade of his knife and smashed it. He dropped it into the vegetables she was stirring.

"As to words," he continued, "I know we use them carelessly. We misuse them, but they're all we've got."

She wondered how much it had cost him to reach this state of equilibrium. She longed for it for herself, but it had eluded her. Probably because her life hadn't included many people she could trust and fewer she had loved. That wasn't surprising, since trust had to exist before love could.

"What are you thinking? That my cracker-barrel philosophy is simplistic?"

"No. I envy you. I don't think many people can state what they believe so succinctly. I know I can't."

"You will. I just have a few years on you, that's all."

While he talked, Quentin removed a container of prepared salad greens from the refrigerator and dumped them into a wooden bowl. He tossed the leaves with a pale golden dressing. Then he set the table.

"Let's see if the pasta is done," he said, returning to the stove. Quentin fished out one long strand. He blew on it briefly before he bit off a piece and chewed it slowly. "Just about right. Here, tell me what you think." He lifted the strand toward her mouth.

Taking food from his hand was the most intimate

thing they'd shared. It was also a test of trust, Merrilee realized. Since he was more introspective than she was and probably more knowledgeable in psychology, undoubtedly he was fully aware of the implication of the gesture. Slowly she leaned forward, opening her mouth to accept the food he offered. She chewed it slowly before she pronounced it done.

It was a relief when Quentin picked up the pot and moved it to the sink to drain it. Increasingly she found it difficult to stand so close to him and pretend his nearness didn't affect her. She had to distance herself from him. When he took the pan of vegetables, she stepped back and watched him dress the pasta from the safety of the other side of the kitchen.

The first mouthful told her that the dish was delicious. "If you ever decide to change careers, don't sell insurance or hide on top of Laurel Mountain. Become a chef. I guarantee, you'll be successful."

"Thanks."

Quentin was obviously pleased by her praise. They ate in comfortable silence. After a while Merrilee laid down her fork with a satisfied sigh. "This gives comfort food new meaning."

"Ready to trade in your Moon Pies and cola for this?" he teased.

"You aren't going to forget that, are you?" When he merely grinned at her, she said, "I could be tempted to make a switch."

Smilingly they faced each other across the table.

"Should I make coffee?"

"Not for me. I'm perfectly contented as I am."

Merrilee's statement was followed by the ringing of Quentin's phone.

"Slow down, Peggy. I can't understand what you're saying." Quentin listened. Then he turned, putting his body between Merrilee and the telephone as if to shield her. "She's with me. You did right to call me. We'll be there in minutes."

When Quentin hung up and turned to face Merrilee, she felt her heart squeezed by anxiety. "What happened?"

Chapter Ten

"Peggy wasn't more specific?" Merrilee asked, fastening her seat belt. Quentin had told her only the bare minimum while they hurried out of his house.

"She said they saw someone on your back porch, trying to break into your house. Howard grabbed one of his handguns and rushed out his back door, yelling bloody murder. The intruder got away. Which is probably just as well. Howard could have gotten himself hurt. Or worse."

"I asked him to call 911 if he saw anything suspicious, but I suspect he considers that an unmanly thing to do," Merrilee said and sighed.

"I'll have a talk with him about playing the Lone Ranger." Quentin turned on the squad car's flashing lights. He negotiated the twisting road down the mountain competently but at a speed that caused Merrilee's eyes to blink nervously a number of times.

Officer Bob Lee Taylor's patrol car was parked in front of Merrilee's house. As soon as Quentin pulled up behind him, the deputy got out of the car, followed by Peggy and Howard. During the next few seconds the Farmers talked simultaneously. Quentin finally calmed them down enough to get answers to his questions.

"Who saw the intruder first?"

"I did," Peggy said. "Ever since Merrilee saw that vagrant or intruder the other night, I've made it my business to look out the kitchen window several times each evening."

"More like every five minutes," Howard added in an aside.

Peggy fixed her husband with stern eyes. "Well, a good thing that I did." Then she turned back to Quentin. "Well, I switched off the kitchen light so I could see better. The moon's quite bright. First, I noticed that Merrilee's porch light was out, which seemed strange to me, because it's the kind that comes on by itself when it gets dark. I thought maybe the bulb burned out or something." She shrugged.

"While I was wondering if I should ask Howard to check the light, I saw somebody move on the porch. He must have been there the whole time, but I didn't see him until he moved. So I called Howard. First he didn't believe me." Peggy cast an accusing look in her husband's direction but gave him no chance to justify himself. "When the man moved around on the porch again, Howard saw him too. He fetched his gun and ran out."

Howard had waited impatiently for this moment. As

soon as Peggy paused for a breath, he jumped in. "I was all fired up, thinking it was the same guy who popped me one the other night," he said, fingering his still slightly swollen lip. "So I ran out yellin' and cussin' like I'd nipped some quart juice. Well, the fellow took off around the house lickety-split. By the time I got up front, he was gone. By then I knew it wasn't the same guy, but it was too late. I'm sorry. I shouldn't have hollered but crept up on him quiet-like, but I was hotter than a two-dollar pistol."

"What makes you think it wasn't the same man?" Quentin asked, even though he knew for a fact that it couldn't have been the same intruder.

"Well, he seemed shorter, skinnier, faster. And he ran funny."

"Funny? In what way?" Quentin wanted to know.

Howard shrugged. "Sort of . . . I don't know. Small steps. Prissy. Funny."

"Can you describe what he wore?"

"Dark pants and a dark coat. And a cap. You know, one of them knitted ones."

"Can you remember anything else?"

"He carried a bag."

"What kind of bag?"

"Come to think of it, it looked more like a sack. You know, the kind chicken feed used to come in? Woven out of hemp or something like that."

"Thanks. Wait right here. The deputy and I will look around." Quentin retrieved a flashlight from the squad car. Both men took off in the direction of Merrilee's backyard.

"What I can't figure out is why somebody would want to break into your house," Peggy said. "It's practically empty except for the piano, which is too big to steal. You got valuable jewelry?"

"Nothing that would bring a decent price in a pawnshop."

"You reckon it's the same person who's trying to make you leave town?"

"Probably."

They stood in worried silence until Quentin and the deputy returned. Bob Lee carried something that looked like a thick stick or an ax handle. He'd wrapped a handkerchief around it to preserve fingerprints. When he reached the car, she saw that there was a hook at the end of the stick.

"What's that?" she asked. When Quentin didn't answer right away, she added, "You may as well tell me. If you don't, I'll worry about it all night and come up with an answer that's a lot scarier than the truth you're hiding."

Quentin seemed to weigh her statement before he spoke. "We're not sure, but we think it's a tool used in handling snakes."

A small cry escaped Merrilee's lips. She pressed the back of her hand over her mouth as if to force further cries back down her throat.

"Somebody tried to jimmy your back door, and one pane in the kitchen window is broken. My guess is, when he couldn't force the door, he broke the window. That's when you two must have seen him. And earlier he'd removed the bulb from the porch light."

"Son of a gun," Howard muttered.

"We'll look around inside, but I don't want you to sleep here tonight," Quentin told Merrilee. "The intruder is getting bolder."

Or more desperate. Aloud she said, "Tonight I'll go to a motel, but tomorrow I'm having an alarm system installed. I don't care how much it costs. Is there somebody in town who can do it?"

"No, but I'll call the Lexington company that the bank used for their new system," Quentin said.

"I guess I'll check into the Holiday Inn."

"You'll do no such thing. You'll use our spare room. Won't she, Howard?"

He nodded. "You'll be safe with us. I'll give you my Lugar to put under your pillow, and I'll keep this baby by my bed." Howard patted the butt of the pistol he'd stuck into his waistband.

"Thanks, you two." Merrilee was touched by the spontaneous, caring hospitality the Farmers offered her. Looking at Quentin, she asked, "May I get a few things from the house?"

"Sure. Come with us."

"We'll go ahead to get the room ready and fix hot chocolate. You look like you could use a cup to warm you up," Peggy said to Merrilee.

"Thanks. That would be great."

While Bob Lee took a piece of plywood from the patrol car to nail into place over the broken pane, Quentin asked Merrilee to stay just inside the door while he checked the whole house.

When he found her standing motionless in the same

spot where he'd left her and saw her fear-rounded eyes, his body tightened with impotent anger. As gently as he could, he explained. "The intruder didn't have time to cut the screen, so nothing could have gotten into the house. I'm double-checking out of habit. That's all."

Thinking of the snake stick, she saw in her mind's eye the contents of the bag writhe and wriggle. Deep loathing and fear cut to her very bone marrow.

"Don't," Quentin said softly, laying both hands on her shoulders. "Don't dwell on it." Conscious of Bob Lee's approaching footsteps, he quickly squeezed her shoulders before he dropped his hands.

"The window's fixed. I'll get a lightbulb from Mr. Farmer for the porch light." Bob Lee nodded politely to Merrilee and left.

Forcing herself into action, Merrilee ran upstairs to gather a few toiletries, a nightgown, and a change of clothes.

Quentin took her arm as they silently walked toward her neighbor's house. When they neared the back door, Quentin said, "You must think I'm a real hick-town cop who can't find his rear end in the dark."

"No, I don't. Nobody could have found the person harassing me because there hasn't been anything concrete to go on. You have nothing to blame yourself for. You're doing all that's possible to do."

"You're quite something, you know that?"

Merrilee perceived the wonder in Quentin's voice. It thrilled her, and for the first time since they left his house, a little of the good feeling she'd enjoyed there returned. Before Quentin could say anything else, Peggy flung the back door open, catching them in the light spilling from the kitchen.

"Come on in. The hot chocolate is waiting. I made a cup for you too, Quentin."

"Thanks, but I can't stay. There are a couple of things I have to do yet tonight." Quentin bid them good night and disappeared into the dark.

"You're seeing a lot of Quentin these days," Peggy said as the two women sat at the kitchen table, sipping hot chocolate. Howard had opted for a longneck bottle of beer and the wrestling match on the television set in the living room.

Using the pretext of drinking, Merrilee mumbled a noncommittal, "Mmm."

"I take it that means yes?"

"Yes. Aren't you the one who pointed out that Quentin's got a good job, is educated, not ugly, and isn't a drinking man?"

"Oh, I'm not being critical. I think we can add that he's got good manners, which means he was raised right. That's more important than you might think."

Merrilee looked at Peggy, who was just waiting to explain that statement. "How's that?"

"It means that once that first rush of heat's gone, when you don't feel all feather-legged no more, he'll still treat you good. You know, gentle-like, and not like some redneck yahoo who gets lickered up and slaps you around regular."

"Peggy, slow down. All Quentin did was cook supper for me."

"Is he a good cook?"

"Yes."

Peggy nodded, pleased. "That's a good sign. He knows what women's work is like, so he'll appreciate all you do." She drained her cup before she asked, "You ain't against marriage, are you?"

"No, but that doesn't mean I'm ready to jump into matrimony either."

"If you don't mind my saying so, you ain't exactly a spring chick no more."

Merrilee grimaced. "Thanks a lot, Peggy."

"I'm only talking to you like this because you don't have no ma. You know I got your best interests at heart."

"I know. I promise I'll give marriage some thought."

"Good. I always worried that Willadean turned you against matrimony. She didn't think much of men. By the way, I've been meaning to ask you. How long are you staying in Browne's Station?"

"Until spring."

"That's enough time for a proper courting."

"Providing somebody doesn't succeed in slipping a poisonous snake into my bed."

"Hush! Don't even think that. We'll get whoever is doing that, don't you worry none. That reminds me. Ma was clearheaded this afternoon. I asked her about the serpent-handling church in Mt. Hebron. She said they were active until the state outlawed it. She couldn't remember the year. She also said some preachers kept their snakes and used them on the sly."

"Did she remember any names?"

Peggy nodded. "It seems the women of the Jennings family were famous for snake-handling, especially one called Sister Sula. Ma also told me that they kept a Mason jar of poisonous liquid by the altar for those members who wanted to drink it to prove their faith. They used natural poisons from plants. Crazy, ain't it?"

"To say the least. Didn't anybody ever die?"

"Some did. There's a lot of weirdness in this world."

After a while Howard joined them. As promised, he brought one of his handguns, which he insisted Merrilee place under her pillow. To please him, she did.

She had feared that it would take her a long time to fall asleep and that her sleep would be filled with nightmares, but her fears were unfounded. Out of emotional exhaustion, she fell asleep quickly and remained so. She awoke refreshed and filled with determination to find answers to the puzzling events plaguing her life.

Before visiting her aunt later that day, Merrilee stopped at the Flower Mart for a potted plant to replace the floral arrangement she'd sent days earlier to the nursing home. She selected a huge pot of mums whose sunshine-bright yellow petals would cheer up Aunt Hazel's drab corner.

While she waited for the clerk to wrap the container in green foil, Merrilee walked through the store, looking at the knickknacks displayed on the tall glass shelves. Gradually she became aware of furtive movements on the other side of the display. It seemed to her that the shadowy shape she saw there ducked down and moved only when she moved. Intrigued, she wondered who was trying to avoid her. Before she could decide on a strategy, the clerk's voice called a name that solved the mystery.

"Mrs. Smith? Where are you?"

At first there was nothing but silence from the other side. Then, apparently realizing that she had no choice but to come forward, the shadowy shape straightened up and scurried to the service desk. With quick steps Merrilee followed Della.

"Here's the centerpiece. I hope Miz Buford'll like it. Big party up to the house?" the clerk asked.

"Yes, Mr. Mainwright's coming to stay for a few days." Della bent to sign the charge slip.

"Oh, the lieutenant governor himself. He sounds like a good man. I think I'll vote for him." The clerk adjusted a carnation in the flower arrangement.

"Hello, Della." Merrilee was startled by the way Della jumped as if she'd jabbed her with a needle. The cook's face drained of what little color it had possessed. Why was the woman so nervous around her? It was more than nerves, judging from Della's panicky eyes. The woman seemed to be afraid of her.

"Hey," Della finally said, licking her dry lips. Her fingers trembled when she reached for the showy arrangement.

The other clerk brought Merrilee the potted plant. Having caught Della alone, Merrilee decided to exploit the opportunity. Hurrying after the thin figure, Merrilee caught up with the cook at the door.

"Here, let me open the door, since you've got your hands full. That is certainly a stunning arrangement."

Della seemed to be anything but pleased to find Merrilee at her side but didn't know what to do about it. She walked as rapidly as her load allowed her toward the parking lot.

"I've been meaning to come see you," Merrilee said.

That remark so startled Della that she stumbled.

"Careful," Merrilee said.

"What . . . what do you want to see me about? I don't know nothin'."

"You knew my mother. It's only natural that I'm curious about her. Now that I've found you, you can tell me everything you know."

Stopping at the station wagon, Della fumbled in her coat pocket for the key.

"Here, let me unlock the door," Merrilee offered. She took the key from Della's hand without waiting for an answer. When they'd placed the centerpiece on the backseat, Merrilee said, "Why don't I buy you a cup of coffee? The Wagon Wheel Cafe is right over there. Just ten minutes. Surely you can take a little break. Knowing Mrs. Buford's reputation, I'm sure she gets more than her money's worth of work from you."

For the first time Della showed some spirit. "You got that right. The woman's a slave driver. 'Della do this, and Della do that,'" she mimicked in a high-pitched voice. "Fetch and carry, fetch and carry, all day long. I have to do things a cook oughtn't have to do. Like picking up the flowers and the dry cleaning and the medicine for Miss Pet."

"Seems to me Mrs. Mainwright could pick up her own medicine, especially on a day when you have to fix a big supper for company. Unless she's sick?"

"Naw, she ain't sick, lessen you count a hang—" Della broke off guiltily. Quickly she added, "I'm just picking up her nerve pills."

It wasn't difficult to finish that first sentence. Did the lieutenant governor's wife have a drinking problem? If so, they'd kept it a secret from the public. Merrilee suspected that if she pressed Della for details, the woman would clam up. "So, what are you fixing for this supper, and who all will be there?"

Della warmed up to the subject, stowed Merrilee's plant on the backseat, and kept talking till they were seated in a booth with two cups of coffee before them.

"Oh, my, that sounds absolutely delicious." Merrilee didn't have to pretend her admiration for the menu. "Do you have anybody to help you, or is it all up to you?"

"Well, Odessa helps some. You know, peels potatoes and such, but she ain't no fancy cook. It's all up to me. I don't mind. It's my job."

"And you're obviously good at it. But a thank you and a compliment now and then would help, wouldn't it?"

Della's face flushed with gratitude for Merrilee's understanding words. "It sure would. But them two women—actually, the whole family except Mr. Mainwright and Miss Crystal—ain't much on thank-yous."

"Who's Miss Crystal?"

"She's Miss Pets and Mr. Mainwright's daughter. Miz Buford's granddaughter."

"Now I remember hearing about her. She's about my age or a little older, but she was always somewhere back East at a fancy girls' school, so I never saw her. Who else is at the house?"

"Mr. Deke. He's Miz Buford's son who runs the businesses in town. The Lincoln car dealership."

Della seemed relaxed enough for Merrilee to risk asking about the past. Very casually and with an encouraging smile, she said, "Tell me about my mother. When did you first meet her?"

"We sang in the choir together. Over at the church. She had a real nice voice, nice enough to get to sing solos."

"Was my mother married when you met her?"

"Oh, no. She was working the switchboard at the Buford Bank then. She was a popular girl. All the guys had a yen for her. Even the married ones. Kept pestering her, but Mr. Mainwright always protected her. She only got married later, when she—" Della blushed and broke off.

"When she what?"

"When she met your father."

Merrilee could have sworn that that wasn't what Della had almost said earlier. Before she could pursue that thought, Della fumbled in her purse for money.

"I really have to go," she said.

"This is my treat." Merrilee placed money on the table. She'd have to ask some questions on their way back to the parking lot. "I guess my mother moved into the cabin near you after she got married?"

"Oh, no. She moved out to Piney Creek Hollow while she was working at the bank. When I first met her, she lived in Miller's rooming house. She hated it. Said there weren't no privacy. Back then there was hardly any apartments for rent in town," Della explained.

Merrilee nodded encouragingly.

"So, when I told her about the cabin's being empty, she took it real quick. It weren't fancy, but it was clean, and the rent was reasonable. Still, it surprised me some, her being a single woman and all, wanting to live out there in the woods. Later on it made sense, her wanting privacy."

Della broke off, her face mirroring a mixture of slyness and alarm at what she had revealed.

"Why did she want privacy?"

Della shrugged and reached for a tissue to blow her nose. Merrilee knew she was stalling for time to prepare an answer.

"I reckon she wanted the privacy for . . . courting."

Was Della implying that Merrilee's parents had slept together before they were married? That hardly shocked Merrilee, but thirty years ago that kind of behavior wouldn't have been accepted in a small town as readily as it was now. "Are you saying they lived together?"

"Mercy, no! Folks didn't do that sort of thing back then in Browne's Station. No, Rafe didn't move in until they'd pledged their vows right and proper."

"What was my dad like?" When Della seemed nonplussed, Merrilee repeated, "My dad? Rafe Ingram?"

"Oh. He was handsome. And footloose. To tell you the truth, it surprised me some that Reba got him to marry her. I always thought he weren't the marrying kind. I guess you never know who or what it takes to get a man to the altar."

That certainly seemed an odd statement. Merrilee didn't know what to make of it. They'd reached the station wagon. This was her last chance to ask about that mysterious car Della had seen the night of the fire.

"I believe you about the car you saw that night, you know. You're not the kind of woman who would imagine almost being run over. Otis might not believe you, but I do."

Della eyed Merrilee dubiously. It was clear she was glad someone believed her, but she was also thinking about her bossy husband. "I'll bet you even remember what kind of car it was. You know, whether it was a sedan or a coupe or a truck—"

"It wasn't no truck. It was a sedan. A dark one."

"A big, expensive sedan?"

Della nodded.

"A Cadillac maybe?"

"No."

"A Chrysler? A Lincoln?"

Della looked uncertain.

"Try to think back. Recall the car coming toward you. Did you jump back?"

"Yes."

"Okay. It passed by. Did you look after it? See the taillights? The cabin was in flames, so there was some light. Think, Della."

"It was a Lincoln. Sure as shootin', it was a Lincoln. I know Lincolns. My brother-in-law was a car salesman who was always showing off the Lincoln he got to buy cheap because it was a demonstration car. Well, I'll be." She seemed dumbfounded that she'd actually remembered the make of the car.

"Anything else you recall about that night?"

"No."

Suddenly Della's anxiety returned. She glanced around furtively as if to see if anyone was watching them.

"What's wrong? Why are you afraid?"

Della blanched. She lowered her eyes but not before Merrilee saw the guilt and the fear mirrored there.

"I gotta go. I'm runnin' late as it is." Della scooted behind the wheel and started the ignition.

Merrilee took her plant from the backseat and stepped away from the car. Della was still holding something back, something that troubled her. Next time she'd get the cook to tell her everything.

Now that she knew what kind of car had been near the burning cabin, how could that help her? More precisely, how could she find out to whom that Lincoln had been registered all those years ago? Every town had an auto license branch. As a matter of fact, she had to go there to get a Kentucky license plate for her car.

Consulting her watch, she realized she would have time to do that before the man from the Lexington security firm was due to inspect the house.

The license branch was located in the basement of the courthouse. The clerk on duty, a bored-looking man in his midtwenties whose face was pitted from adolescent acne, sold her the Kentucky license plate and showed little emotion when Merrilee asked how far back they kept records.

"We got papers back there," the clerk said, pointing a blunt finger toward a storage room, "that go back to World War II. The county clerk doesn't like to throw files out as long as we have room to store them. Now we're putting stuff onto computers."

Merrilee confided in the clerk that she needed to know what sort of cars people drove years ago in a small town like Browne's Station for her next music video. That impressed him sufficiently to lead her to a windowless room lined with tall, gray steel cabinets. She took one drawer of records after another to a small table and started looking for owners of Lincolns.

When she finished a couple of hours later, she had three names: Amos Edwards, Lurlene Buford, and Ferlin Young. Mrs. Buford owned the Lincoln dealership, so it seemed natural for her to drive one of the cars. Dr. Edwards lived on Hickory Drive, and Ferlin Young at the rooming house. Odd. She had never heard of the rooming house until two days ago, and now she'd come across it again. Merrilee wrote down the address, though she doubted that the place still existed.

Chapter Eleven

Outside the courthouse, Merrilee ran into Quentin. They greeted each other with a smile and a friendly hello.

"I went to the courthouse to check on something, and I finally cornered Della. We had a talk."

"Why don't you come to my office and tell me about it?"

In the privacy of his office she related her meeting with Della. And about who had owned Lincoln at the time of the fire. He wrote the names on a notepad on his desk.

"I was wondering what you were doing in the courthouse. Let's see. Dr. Edwards died several years ago. The reason I know that is that I came across his name in some records I looked at. He acted as coroner when the regular coroner was on vacation. From what I know of him, I can't imagine his being at your cabin unless one of you had been sick. Mrs. Buford. She's still with us, and the whole family still drives Lincolns. In fact, they own the dealership in town."

"Is there anything the Bufords don't own around here?"

"In recent years their stranglehold on the town has loosened some, but they still own plenty." Quentin consulted his notepad. "Ferlin Young. Never heard of him." Quentin opened a drawer in his desk and removed a city directory. "He isn't listed, which only means that he didn't live here when the latest city census was taken."

"I also have news about the snake handlers." Merrilee related the information Peggy's mother had revealed.

"That rates a trip to Mt. Hebron."

"When are we going?"

Amused by her enthusiasm, Quentin smiled. "I didn't say anything about your going." Seeing her expression, he lifted a hand to forestall her reply. "Okay, okay. You can come." Quentin consulted his appointment book, then his watch. "The only time I can go today is right now. Are you free?"

"Yes. The glazier fixed the window first thing this morning, and the security systems man won't be there until later. Let's go."

It was a good day for a drive. As they followed the winding road around the base of Laurel Mountain, the sun kept breaking through the clouds, and the brisk wind helped disperse the last remnants of that morning's mist and fog.

"Don't get your hopes up," Quentin warned. "We may find out that all the snake handlers have left. But if we're lucky, we might get some names."

He pulled into the combination filling station and grocery store, which was the only building at the crossroads that showed signs of life. Several cars were parked out front. Across the street a small building featured a sign that read simply, MOM'S EATS.

While Quentin spoke with the woman behind the cash register, Merrilee looked around. The store was incredibly crowded, yet in the middle of it stood a wood-burning stove with several chairs around it in a semicircle. Just then only one old man sat there. Quentin placed his hand on Merrilee's elbow and nudged her toward the man.

"Mr. Wallace, may we speak with you for a moment?"

The man turned his red, rheumy eyes toward them. "Sure thing, son. I got nothing but time. Set, set."

After Quentin introduced Merrilee and himself, they sat down.

"We're trying to find former members of the Mt. Hebron Church. Your daughter-in-law said you might remember names."

Mr. Wallace nodded. "Yup. I used to be the postmaster here when this was a town. Mt. Hebron Holiness Church was a snake cult church with a good-sized congregation. I never held with that kind of worship, but many folks did. Eventually the state put a stop to the serpent handling. Anybody you're particularly interested in?"

"Yes, the Jennings women. Did you know them?"

"Sure did. Sula Jennings was well-known for her talent in charming snakes."

"Do you know what happened to her?"

"Same thing that'll happen to all of us. She died."

"Oh." Another dead end, Merrilee thought sadly.

"Were there younger women who handled the church snakes?" Quentin asked.

"Sula's daughter. From what I heard, she promised to be even better at it than her ma."

Quentin and Merrilee exchanged a guardedly hopeful look. "Do you know what happened to her?"

"Disagreement with her ma over her choice of a boyfriend caused her to move away."

"Do you remember the daughter's name?"

Mr. Wallace thought so long that Merrilee wondered if he'd fallen asleep.

Finally he spoke. "No, I can't recollect it, but it was an old-timey kind of a name. Both of her names were, but she didn't like one of them. When she was older, she told everybody to call her by her other name. I reckon that should have been our first hint that she wasn't that sweet thing she pretended to be."

"Can you estimate how old the daughter would now be?" Quentin asked.

"She must be in her fifties."

"Can you describe her?" Merrilee asked.

"I can do better than that, young lady." He called to the front of the store. "Emmy, bring me my Mt. Hebron picture album." He turned back to them. "It'll take but a moment. We live behind the store. Photography used to be a hobby of mine in my younger days. Took pictures of most of the folks who lived around here."

Emmy brought a thick album and placed it in the old man's lap. He put on a pair of wire-rimmed glasses and opened the album with a gesture that was both reverent and ceremonious.

"Let's see. Oh, look at that. The centennial celebration of our town. Everybody turned out for that." Entranced, he looked at the photos for a minute before he turned the page. "Here's the memorial we erected in memory of our brave boys who died in the war. And here's our new fire engine and volunteers."

Merrilee wondered how many years of photos they'd have to look at before they got to the snake women.

Very gently Quentin said, "Mr. Wallace, you were going to show us the Jennings women."

"I was?" The old man looked surprised. After blinking a couple of times, he said, "That's right. The Mt. Hebron Holiness Church and serpent handlers. Now I remember." He began turning the pages more quickly. "Ah, here we are. That's Sula."

Merrilee bent closer. Mr. Wallace pointed to a photo showing a middle-aged woman facing the camera head-on. The teenager, unfortunately, had her head turned so that it was impossible to recognize her features.

"The older woman seems very familiar to me," Merrilee said, excited. "I know I've seen her before."

"Where? When?" Quentin asked.

"I don't know, but I'm positive I've seen that face.

Do you have a better photo of the daughter?" she asked Mr. Wallace.

He turned the page. Merrilee drew back with a gasp and averted her eyes.

"Easy," Quentin said. He placed a hand on her arm.

"Yeah, I remember that now. The girl sort of poked the snake at me. Caused me to jump back too. I never was real fond of snakes, so I didn't take but the one picture of her."

He looked thoughtfully at the photo and shook his head. "She was a strange one, with a sly, mean streak in her. She appeared meek and biddable, but she was a wily one."

Quentin handed his card to Mr. Wallace. "If you remember the woman's name or anything else about her, please call me collect."

They thanked the old man and left him pondering the photo history of his town.

"Don't look so down, Merrilee. We knew this might be a wild goose chase." When she didn't reply, Quentin pointed to the restaurant across the highway. "How about a cup of coffee?"

"Why not? I've never been in a place called Mom's Eats."

"Neither have I."

The restaurant turned out to be an old-fashioned diner. A truck driver sat at one end of the long counter, drinking coffee. Two-tiered glass display cases filled with donuts, slabs of pie, and triangles of dark chocolate cake thickly iced with milk chocolate frosting sat at regular intervals on the counter.

"That looks good," Quentin told the waitress, pointing to a wedge of lemon meringue pie. "How about you, Merrilee? Join me in some comfort food?"

Merrilee ordered the chocolate cake with her coffee. "You realize, don't you, that if we don't find out soon who's doing this to me, I'll weigh a ton and won't fit into a seat on the tour bus?"

Her joking didn't fool Quentin. He gazed at her, his eyes somber. "This is getting to you, isn't it?"

Merrilee shrugged. "It's getting harder not to worry about what'll happen next."

"We'll get him. Or her. It's only a matter of time. Trust me." Noting her smile, he asked, "What's amusing?"

"I'm sorry. It's just that every time a man says 'trust me' to a woman on the afternoon soap operas, awful things start to happen to her."

"Let me rephrase that. Rely on me. Is that better?"

"Only marginally."

"It made you smile, and that's something."

The waitress served them. For the next few minutes they concentrated on the food.

"Is your cake good?"

"It's delicious. Want a taste?"

"Sure." Quentin faced her, obviously waiting.

A little surprised that he'd taken her up on her offer, Merrilee speared a chunk with her fork and lifted it to his mouth.

"You're right. This is good and chocolaty, just the way I like it. Want to try some of my lemon pie?"

She shook her head. "I don't want anything to lessen

this double-chocolate taste. If my hips are going to get wider and wider, the least I want to do is enjoy the process."

Quentin leaned back, pretending to study her jeans-clad hips. "You've got a long way to go before we can even begin to speak of wide," he pronounced solemnly, but a grin tugged at his mouth.

"I hope so. The only time in my life I've had to diet is when I shot a music video. I had to lose ten pounds. I didn't like dieting." In a lower voice she added, "And speaking of not liking something, look who's coming in."

Glancing at the mirrored wall, Quentin watched Sheriff Chapman's approach.

"Well, I knew from your car outside that I'd find you here, Chief, but I didn't know I'd have the pleasure of seeing you again, Miss Ingram."

"Hello, Sheriff Chapman." Quentin nodded to his fellow officer, who promptly sat down beside him.

"Heard you had a murder in town. I must have just left the cemetery when y'all found him." Wiley Chapman signaled the waitress.

"That's right," Quentin said, finishing his pie.

"Found out who the victim is yet?"

"No."

"Well, it's probably just some vagrant passing through."

"Could be," Quentin said.

"He'll probably never be missed, so you don't have to bust a gut trying to find out who did it. More'n likely it was just another bum. Got into an argument over something. A bottle of cheap wine or a blanket, maybe. I had a case once where two of them got into a knife fight over a candy bar. I'll bet that's what happened, a fight that got out of hand. Then the survivor carried his victim to the cemetery and gave him a quick burial in the leaves."

"What makes you think he wasn't killed in the grave-yard?"

After a tiny pause, the sheriff said, "Just common sense. Bums wouldn't be hanging out in the cemetery, would they? Nobody does. The murder took place nearby, and the killer thought the graveyard was a good hiding place."

"Probably," Quentin said.

The waitress set a cup of coffee in front of the sheriff. Quentin paid their bill, and after a quick good-bye they left.

When they reached the car, Merrilee said, "The sheriff certainly was interested in the murder. Professional interest?"

"I guess, though he's never been that curious about one of our cases before."

"His theory is all wrong. No vagrant wears the kind of clothes the dead man wore. Why didn't you set him straight on that?"

"Because it's none of his business."

Both were silent for most of the trip back to town.

"I wish I could remember where I saw Sula Jennings."

"Are you sure it was she?"

"As opposed to whom?"

"Someone who looked like her. Remember, in that

photo Sula was already middle-aged, and that was taken years ago."

"You're right," Merrilee agreed. "I couldn't have seen Sula, so it must be someone who looks a lot like her. A relative. Maybe even her daughter." Merrilee closed her eyes, concentrating on the image. "This is driving me crazy. Something's nagging at me, but every time I almost know what it is, I lose it again."

"Don't try so hard, and it'll come to you."

"I hope so."

At the courthouse, Quentin walked her to her car. When she was seated behind the wheel, he invited her out to supper for the following evening. She accepted.

Humming the new melody she had composed, Merrilee drove home, where she found an estimate for the security system and the company owner's promise to have the system installed within two days.

Merrilee was alarmed when she saw Aunt Hazel an hour later. Her aunt's color was bad; her skin looked like the parchment of an ancient manuscript, ready to crumple at the slightest touch. Her lips had a bluish tinge. Although she claimed to feel "passably well," Merrilee suspected that her aunt was in pain.

"Maybe Dr. Albright needs to change your medication. Should I phone him?"

"No. He'll be back tomorrow. I'll talk to him then. I'm just tired, that's all." Seeing her niece's scowl, she continued quickly. "Now that you're here, I feel better already. Thank you for those pretty mums."

Merrilee wasn't that easily distracted. "What did you

do today that you shouldn't have, that tired you out?" From the guilty flush on Hazel's face she knew she'd guessed right.

"I only made a couple of phone calls."

Aunt Hazel was a poor liar.

"What else? Did you have visitors?"

"Oh, just some people."

When Hazel couldn't meet her niece's eyes, Merrilee knew. "Oh, no! Aunt Hazel, you promised you wouldn't see the Cosgroves again—"

"Don't be angry with me," Hazel pleaded. "I had to see Brother John and Sister Bridie once more to straighten things out. I told them what I've decided to do. They know my mind's made up, and that's that." Hazel lifted her chin.

"Are you sure they won't bother you again? I can get a restraining order against them."

"That won't be necessary. It's settled. I know I made the right decision. I don't care whether Mose would approve or not. Maybe this will make up a little for how I failed you."

"Hush, Aunt Hazel. No more recriminations. I thought we agreed on that. The past's done with. What counts is now. Which brings me to something I've been meaning to discuss with you. As soon as you're well enough to leave here, I want you to come and live with me in my house. Would you like that?"

Tears prevented Hazel from speaking, so she just nodded.

"Good. I'll get a room added on in back so you won't have to climb stairs. I'll be in Browne's Station until next spring. While I'm off recording and touring, I'll hire a housekeeper to take care of you."

"I don't deserve this," Hazel whispered.

"Stop talking like that. We're family, aren't we? We belong together. What do you say? It's not a fancy house, but it's comfortable."

"Fancy doesn't matter to me. And I can pay for the room addition. I've got money."

"So have I. Now then, will you move in with me?"

Hazel nodded shyly, her eyes shining with happy tears.

Merrilee smiled. "Good. That's settled."

A nurse entered, interrupting their conversation. "Here's your milk shake, honey, and your pills," she said cheerily. "Now don't you make a face. You've got to get your strength up. Those Cosgroves plumb wore you out."

Anger narrowed Merrilee's eyes into slits. "What did they do?"

"I don't know exactly, except they hollered and upset your aunt something awful. We had to give her some of her heart medicine real quick after Glady's threw . . . asked them to leave."

"The pills will make me fall asleep, and I have company," Hazel protested weakly.

"Visiting hours are over until tonight. Now it's time for your afternoon nap," the nurse said firmly.

Seeing Hazel's disappointed look, Merrilee asked, "May I stay with my aunt until she falls asleep?"

"I'll make you a deal," the nurse said, placing a pill in Hazel's hand and offering her some water. "You get your aunt to drink all her shake, and you can stay till she's asleep."

"You've got a deal." Merrilee did as she had promised. Hazel didn't like the shake but drank it dutifully. All the time Merrilee bit down her anger.

"I talked with a former neighbor of ours who claimed that my mother had a lovely singing voice. I hadn't known that."

"Reba sang like an angel. Your voice is a lot like hers."

"So both my parents had musical talent. No wonder I never wanted to do anything but sing."

"There's something I've been mulling over in my mind about telling you." Hazel yawned. "Sorry. The pills work fast."

"About my parents?"

"Yes."

Merrilee waited.

"Maybe I shouldn't. Then I think, what if you have a family of your own one day? You might need to know."

Hazel's voice was fading fast. Merrilee bent down close. "What do you want to tell me?"

"Something your mama wrote me. Your daddy . . ."

"Yes? What about my dad?"

"Wasn't . . . who you think. . . ." Hazel's voice trailed off.

Merrilee waited, but she was losing her aunt to the powerful sedative. Hazel struggled to keep her eyes open but couldn't. And Merrilee wasn't sure just what she'd said.

"You can tell me some other time, Aunt Hazel. Don't

try to talk now. Sleep." Merrilee doubted that her aunt even heard her. She kissed the pale cheek.

Ethel Mae's bed was still empty. At the front desk she found out that she'd been taken to the hospital for tests.

"About your aunt's visitors," Gladys began, looking uncomfortable. "They sneaked in when we were away from the desk for a minute, tending a patient. It was an emergency. I've hired someone who'll do nothing but stay at this desk and check everybody coming in. The Cosgroves won't get in to see your aunt again."

Merrilee believed her. "Did anyone overhear what the argument was about?"

"Ethel Mae heard part of it. She thought they were badgering her about money."

"I can't believe they'd stoop so low as to hassle an old, sick woman." Merrilee felt ill with anger.

"It seems a mite low, even for them two," Gladys agreed. "Except Brother John's congregation isn't nearly as big as it used to be, so he could be hurting for money."

Merrilee thought this over on the way to the parking lot. Of all the things she held against John Cosgrove, and she held plenty, being mercenary wasn't one of them. Bridie, however, was greedy. Suddenly Merrilee stopped as if hit by lightning. The image shimmered crystal bright in her mind.

Merrilee knew who looked like Sula Jennings, the snake woman.

Chapter Twelve

Merrilee's elation faded fast. Now that she realized who reminded her of Sula Jennings's photo, she scarcely knew what to do with that information. It didn't seem to help at all in explaining who was terrorizing her, and yet . . . She shook her head, trying to clear it, but it didn't help. Merrilee started her car, but, still thinking of her problem, she ignored the car's reminder to fasten her seat belt.

The powerful heater of the Mercedes kicked on. Moments later Merrilee felt the heat blow around her feet. In response she slipped out of her open-toed sling pumps and flexed her cold feet. She drove slowly, absentmindedly enjoying the warmth. She had just pulled out onto the highway when she thought she caught a movement out of the corner of her eye.

Turning her head to her right, her eyes zeroed in on

the shape coming to life on the passenger side of the car. Mesmerized, she watched the shape slither onto the floor. Time froze. From far off she heard someone whimper, the kind of whimper that made her scalp tighten in terror. Almost as if this were happening to someone else, her brain registered the car's crashing into a thicket, perceived the door flying open and her body being flung through the air. Then everything went dark.

Sometime later, sounds, distorted and distant, tried to break through to her mind.

"Easy. Easy. Move her very carefully."

The voice seemed familiar to Merrilee.

"Chief, we've handled accident victims before."

Hands touched her, lifted her. When the back of her head came into contact with something, she cried out in pain. She sank once more into the welcoming darkness of the soothing waves.

The next time Merrilee became aware of her surroundings, she was propelled into consciousness suddenly, brutally, painfully. This time she knew she cried out when she was lifted up and deposited onto a firm surface.

"My head," she whispered. Merrilee lifted her left hand, intending to touch her head, but the pain shooting through her shoulder prevented her from completing the gesture.

"We'll take a look at your shoulder in a minute," the doctor said in response to her groan. Though his fingers were gentle when he touched the back of her head, Merrilee flinched.

"That's a good-sized bump you've got there, but the skin isn't broken, so we won't have to shave your head to put in stitches."

That was good news, but the pain radiating from the lump was too intense for Merrilee to be properly appreciative. She answered the doctor's questions as best as she could. Stoically she submitted to being poked, prodded, and patted. The only time she responded audibly was when he examined the left side of her rib cage.

"We'll take an X-ray," he said, "because there's a chance one or two of your ribs might be cracked."

Alarmed, Merrilee's eyes flew open. She shut them immediately, for the overhead light was so bright.

Sensing her alarm, the doctor assured her that even if the ribs were broken, it wasn't a serious condition. She was transported through endless-seeming halls. And between being undressed and X-rayed, she kept dozing off.

"Merrilee, what happened?"

Reluctantly she opened her eyes to look at Quentin, who was bending over her. His face seemed grim. "I don't know," she murmured, wanting only to escape into sleep.

"Can't you remember anything?"

"It's not unusual for someone with a concussion not to remember right away what happened immediately prior to the injury," the doctor said.

The two men talked some more, but Merrilee felt too bruised and exhausted to listen. She thought she heard the word *snake*. The next thing she knew, a nurse drew the curtain around the bed and proceeded to examine her.

After a while Merrilee heard her say, "I don't see any evidence of a bite. By now the site would be red and swollen." Through the night they kept checking her vital signs despite Merrilee's feeble protests. All she wanted was to sleep.

"Looks like she's waking up."

"It's about time. I was getting worried."

"No need to. I told you we would monitor her condition."

Merrilee kept her eyes closed, debating whether she wanted to sleep some more or ask questions. Her curiosity won. Opening her eyes, she surveyed the two men standing by her bed. One of them she knew; the other she thought was the doctor.

"I was about to wake you," Quentin said.

"What stopped you? Everybody else did just that all night long."

"How do you feel?"

"I think I could do an award-winning headache commercial."

The doctor wrote something on a chart, which he hung on the foot of the bed. "The nurse will bring you something that should relieve the pain. Let me look at your eyes."

After he finished the examination, she asked, "What's wrong with my head?"

"You have a concussion. Luckily it's only a mild one. In a day or two you'll be as good as new. I'll see you tomorrow." With a nod to both of them, the physician left.

Relieved, Merrilee placed the palms of her hands flat against the mattress, attempting to push herself up into a sitting position. She collapsed with a groan. Before the pain subsided, perspiration beaded on her forehead. Quentin fetched a warm, wet washcloth from the bathroom and bathed her face gently.

"Nothing's broken, but you sure are bruised. Do you remember anything of what happened?"

"Nothing."

"From what I've pieced together, you lost control of your car and ran off the road. Luckily yesterday's rain had turned the shoulder into pure, soft mud. That and some bushes slowed the car down enough so that when you rammed into a tree, the impact was considerably diminished. You were thrown from the car and apparently landed on your left side. In the process, you hit your head."

"What made me lose control of the car? Did a tire blow?"

"No. I've had the Mercedes towed to a garage and gone over by experts. There was nothing wrong with it."

"Then what? I was clean and sober. I'm not given to fainting spells. I don't remember braking for an animal. Did someone run me off the road?"

"In a manner of speaking."

"Quentin, what does that mean?"

"I'd rather not say. I need you to remember what happened."

"Gladly, but how do I do that?"

"Are you willing to try something unorthodox?"

"At this point I'll try just about anything."

Quentin rubbed his chin. Looking closer, Merrilee realized he hadn't shaved. The stubble on his face was several shades darker than the blond hair on his head. His face was drawn, weary, his uniform slightly rumpled. She wondered if he'd gotten any sleep. Before she could ask, he spoke.

"I've talked to a specialist I know. He said that you will probably remember what happened in time, but time is the one thing I'm convinced we don't have. I want to stop the escalating harassment."

He paused, as if choosing his words carefully.

"Go on," Merrilee encouraged. "What did the specialist recommend?"

"He wants you to try hypnosis."

Merrilee gulped. "Hypnosis? I thought maybe he'd want to administer sodium pentothal or whatever the truth serum's scientific name is."

"Not remembering is not the same as lying. Merrilee, hypnosis is an accepted, respected tool in psychiatry. It was used in the VA hospital where I worked." She seemed uncertain. "You don't have to go through with it if you still have any doubts after talking with the doctor. Just hear him out."

"You really think it's that important that I remember what happened as quickly as possible?"

"Yes." Quentin sat on the bed and took her hand in his. "You were extremely lucky yesterday. You could have been seriously injured, maybe even killed. It's one thing to send nuisance letters, but something quite different to cause someone's car to run off the road."

"Is that what he or she meant to do?"

"I think so."

Again Quentin seemed to weigh his words carefully. Merrilee tensed as she waited.

"Exactly what can you recall of yesterday?"

"Everything until I left the nursing home. Then nothing until the paramedics picked me up."

"Gladys Vernon told me she looked out the window when you left and saw you come to a complete stop, as if you'd suddenly remembered something."

"I don't recall that." Then she asked the question that had worried her for some time. "Do you think the accident was a deliberately planned attempt on my life?" There was only a momentary flicker in Quentin's eyes, but it confirmed her suspicions. "That's what I thought. But why? I swear I haven't done anything to anybody to make them want me dead."

"I believe you. I've taken the liberty of asking Dr. Harrison to come right after lunch. He spends a couple of days a month here in Browne's Station. Are you up to talking to him?"

"He's the psychiatrist?" When Quentin nodded, she said, "Yes. I don't have any choice. If someone is trying to kill me, I'd better find out why. Maybe I'll remember something that might shed light on the identity of the person who's after me."

"I think it's a wise decision to see him. But now I'd better go. I'm tiring you," Quentin said.

"It wouldn't hurt you to get some rest too."

He squeezed her hand. "I'll be back with Dr. Harrison."

Merrilee slept some more. When she awoke, Peggy was sitting by her bed, her big, black, shiny plastic pocketbook resting in her lap, her hands folded over it.

"How're you feeling?" Without waiting for an answer, Peggy rushed on. "You sure gave us a good scare. When Quentin stopped by the house to tell us you'd been in a car accident, Howard and me rushed right over to the hospital, but the doctor wouldn't let us see you." She paused to catch her breath.

"What on earth happened? I know you're a fine, safe driver. Howard taught you good. Why, you never even scratched a fender when you first started to drive Willadean's big Oldsmobile. So what happened yesterday?"

"I don't know. Getting my head bumped made me forget, but my memory loss is only temporary. Or so the doctor claims."

Saucer-eyed, Peggy stared at Merrilee. "Well, don't that beat all. You've got the amnesia. There was a movie on the TV about a woman who had amnesia. She couldn't even remember her own husband or her kids." Peggy shook her head in heartfelt sympathy. "She only remembered when she got knocked out again."

"I don't have that kind of amnesia," Merrilee quickly assured Peggy. She didn't want to tempt her friend into trying the movie's remedy on her.

"How soon will you remember? Did the doctor say?"

"No, but a psychiatrist is going to hypnotize me this afternoon. Maybe that'll restore my memory."

"Land's sake, girl! Hypnotize? You sure that's safe and decent?"

Peggy seemed genuinely worried as well as scandalized, so Merrilee told her that Quentin would be present during the whole procedure.

"Well, that's different. As long as you've got Quentin with you, that doctor will think twice before he tries to plant some improper notions in your mind while he's got you under his spell."

If her head hadn't hurt so, Merrilee would have chuckled.

"Well, since you'll be having visitors soon, it's a good thing I brought you some of your things." Peggy reached for the brown bag sitting on the floor. "I brought your pretty pajamas. The hospital gowns they give people are a disgrace. Why, they ain't hardly decent."

Merrilee accepted Peggy's help. In the bathroom she brushed her teeth and washed her face before exchanging the hospital gown for her emerald-green silk pajamas. She brushed her hair, but each time the brush pulled a strand, pain radiated to her brain. She stopped after a halfhearted attempt to tame the tangles.

When the nurse came with Merrilee's next dose of medication, Peggy left, promising to return that evening. Whatever was in the pills made her fall asleep again, but it also lessened her headache. By noon she was free of nausea. Thirstily she drank the ginger ale the nurse brought her.

As promised, Quentin and Dr. Harrison arrived after lunch. Quentin had shaved, and his khaki uniform was crisp and fresh, though his eyes were red and weary. Merrilee doubted that he'd gotten any sleep.

The psychiatrist wore dark-rimmed glasses that kept sliding down his nose. His chin was covered with a brown and gray beard. His manner was low-key and trust-inspiring.

He sat on the right side of her bed, while Quentin took the chair on the left side.

"Do you have any questions?" Dr. Harrison asked after a straightforward explanation of the process.

"From what you said, not everyone can be hypnotized. What if I'm one of those who can't be?"

He smiled at her reassuringly. "Don't worry about it. Relax. Are you ready?"

Merrilee glanced at Quentin, who gave her a jaunty thumbs-up sign. She took a deep breath. "I'm ready."

The initial emptying-of-the-mind exercises Dr. Harrison led her through were a lot like the quiet period of complete concentration she practiced before going on-stage. Slowly his pleasant voice led her into a state of consciousness where a part of her seemed to float somewhere above her body, looking down on the proceedings.

"Merrilee, you're in the parking lot of the nursing home where you've just visited your aunt. Tell me what's happening, what you're feeling."

"I'm angry because the Cosgroves have been upsetting Aunt Hazel again."

"How are they upsetting your aunt?"

"I don't know exactly, but I think they want money from her."

"You're walking toward your car," Dr. Harrison prompted.

Both men noticed the extraordinary stillness that had come over her. "What are you thinking?"

"I know who Sula Jennings reminded me of earlier today."

"Who?"

"Bridie Cosgrove."

Quentin's left eyebrow arched up, but he remained silent.

"Do you know this Bridie Cosgrove?"

"Yes. She's Sula Jennings' daughter."

"What are you doing now?" Dr. Harrison asked.

"Driving my car."

"Okay. You're now on the highway. What do you see?"

Quentin leaned forward, alarmed by the expression of horror on her face. She whimpered, terrified. The she screamed and threw both arms over her face as if to protect it.

Dr. Harrison brought her out of the hypnosis quickly.

Merrilee panted as if she'd been running a marathon. Her eyes were wild with fear until she realized where she was. She pressed her hands to her sweat-beaded temples.

"I remember now. There was a snake in my car. A copperhead. It had crawled to the front, probably because I'd turned the heater on. Seeing that snake caused me to lose control of the car." Merrilee shuddered.

Then she looked at Quentin. He didn't seem surprised. "You knew about the snake?"

"We found a dead copperhead in the car. When you crashed the passenger side into the tree, it apparently killed the snake."

"I must have forgotten to lock my car. Who'd think something like that could happen in the parking lot of the nursing home?"

"Somebody's aware of your fear of snakes. Who?"

Merrilee shrugged. "Could be anybody who knew Willadean and me in the old days."

"Do you have any idea why you have this phobia?" Dr. Harrison asked.

"No."

"Were you ever bitten by a snake?"

"No."

"How long have you been this afraid of snakes?"

"For as long as I can remember." After being prompted by Quentin, she told the doctor that she hadn't been able to speak right after the fire. Nor could she remember anything of the first five years of her life. "Do you think my phobia is rooted in something that happened then?"

"Do you?"

"Probably," she admitted reluctantly.

"Haven't you ever been tempted to find out why you have no memories of your early life?"

"No. I used to tell the manager of our band, who always urged everyone to go through therapy because she'd done it and swore by it, that most of the band members came from the mountains, where people went to the doctor only when all home remedies had failed. But now I think that was only a convenient excuse. I was . . . I am afraid. I think something really bad happened when I was small."

"Is that just a fear or something more?"

"I have dreams sometimes. Nightmares, actually. I wake up from them, and I'm frightened half out of my mind, but I never know why I'm so frightened."

Dr. Harrison fiddled with a cold pipe he'd taken from his jacket pocket. At last he asked, "Would you like to know why you're so frightened? Once you know, you can fight and conquer that fear. You know that, don't you?"

"Yes, but first I have to face whatever it is that happened. I've never wanted to, thinking that what I don't know can't hurt me. Now Quentin has convinced me, and I think he's right, that the motive behind these attacks on me is rooted in that part of my past I can't remember. Since somebody is trying to kill me, I'd better give therapy a try, even though I don't look forward to it."

"I understand your reluctance. It's only natural under the circumstances, but I'll guide you all the way. You responded well to hypnosis. I'd like to continue using that. Let me warn both of you, though, that this will take time."

"So what else is new?" Merrilee muttered, discouraged.

Ignoring her comment, Quentin asked, "How soon can we start?"

Merrilee was touched by his use of "we" in the

question. He meant to stand by her. She blinked a few times to dispel the moisture that gathered in her eyes. Then she looked at him, not bothering to disguise the emotions she felt.

Dr. Harrison consulted his small appointment book. "Your physician is releasing you in the morning. I could see you tomorrow evening at your house if that's convenient. I'm returning to Lexington the day after that."

Merrilee hesitated for just a beat before she committed herself. "That would be fine. I appreciate your coming to my home." She gave him her address. They talked for a few moments before the psychiatrist left.

Quentin stayed. "I didn't mean to bulldoze you into analysis," he said.

The expression on his face was apologetic, uncertain, as if he had second thoughts about the whole thing. Merrilee reassured him. "It's long overdue. If what happened to me at four had occurred in an urban environment, I'd probably have been put through therapy right after they found me in the woods. The inevitable was only postponed some twenty-six years, that's all."

Merrilee was silent for a moment before she continued thoughtfully. "You know, I think deep down I knew when I returned to Browne's Station that this would be a turning point in my life. Something drove me here."

"Is there anything I can do?"

"As a matter of fact, there is. Butler's furniture store is scheduled to deliver a sofa and a couple of armchairs this afternoon at four. I gave Peggy a key to the house, but I forgot about the furniture delivery when she visited. Could you tell her to let them in?"

"Of course."

Merrilee winced with pain when she sat up straighter. "I seem to be getting stiffer and sorer instead of better."

"It always happens that way. You'll be even sorer in the morning."

Merrilee discovered that Quentin was right when she dressed herself after the doctor discharged her the next morning. Peggy picked her up and drove her home.

The mechanic from the body shop called to say that her car wouldn't be ready for at least a week because they'd had to send for a replacement fender. She would have to rent a car as soon as some of her stiffness wore off.

"I had the deliverymen put the furniture just where Quentin told me to," Peggy said when Merrilee unlocked the front door.

Merrilee looked at her living room. "It looks great." She set the floral bouquet Quentin had sent on the coffee table. The room was ready for Dr. Harrison's visit. She only wished she were.

When the doorbell rang that evening, Merrilee's whole body tensed. The time had come to confront that scary black hole in her past. Would it be like opening Pandora's box?

A tiny voice in her head told her that after tonight's session, nothing would ever be the same again.

Chapter Thirteen

Merrilee sobbed. She shook her head from side to side, her expression pleading. Tears began to pour out from under her closed eyelids. She whimpered in fear. She looked as if she was being sucked into a maelstrom of terror.

Quentin muttered a curse word, but before he could voice his alarm, Dr. Harrison had already started bringing Merrilee out of the trance. It seemed to take a long time.

Unable to remain in his chair any longer, Quentin rushed to the sofa, sat back on his heels, and watched Merrilee's face.

She opened her eyes. "What happened?"

The psychiatrist mopped his face with a handkerchief. "I'm sorry. Everything went fine until I asked you about the night of the fire. Then you became terrified. We'll have to proceed slowly and work our way backward toward that night."

"Do you remember anything?" Quentin asked.

"Yes, but it doesn't make any sense."

"Let me be the judge of that. Something frightened you terribly. Tell me what you remember," Dr. Harrison requested.

"I remember hands. Hands reaching for me."

Both men were silent, waiting for her to continue. When she remained silent, Dr. Harrison asked, "Did the hands reaching for you want to help you?"

"No! Just the opposite. I'm sure of that."

"Describe the hands."

"They were large. Very large."

"The hands of an adult," the doctor said. "A man's or a woman's?"

"A man's."

"What besides their size makes you think they were a man's?" Dr. Harrison asked.

"The knuckles were hairy. The hair was dark."

"Do you remember anything else?"

"No."

"The hands scared you. What else frightened you? There was something else," Dr. Harrison prompted.

Merrilee moistened her dry lips. "Yes. A snake." She hesitated a beat. "The snake was purple."

Both men looked at her, waiting.

"I told you what I remembered didn't make any sense. There's no such thing as a purple snake. At least not in this part of the country."

"Can you describe it?"

"No. I can't," she said, and she shivered. "Except the snake was stylized. Like in a painting. You know, not realistic. I told you it made no sense."

"It's all right," Dr. Harrison said soothingly.

"I'm not sure I can go through anything like this again." Merrilee lifted her hands to look at them. They were trembling. "I feel wiped out." She wrapped her arms around herself.

"Next time we'll approach the problem differently. We'll work our way back slowly, week by week, day by day. I'd like to see you at least once a week. Can you manage that?"

"I suppose." Merrilee didn't feel particularly enthusiastic.

"I understand your reluctance, but nothing as extreme as today will occur again. Each time you confront the memory of that night, some of the negative emotional energy will be drained away. Eventually you'll be able to face the memory without terror." While he consulted his appointment book, the doctor asked, "Do you have anyone who can stay with you tonight?"

"No, but I'm sure the Farmers will let me use their spare room again. Why?"

"You might have nightmares. On the other hand, you might sleep like a baby. It's hard to predict. Can you come a week from today?"

"Yes." Dr. Harrison handed her a card that listed his office address and phone number. He had added his home phone number as well.

After seeing the doctor to the door, Merrilee returned to the living room and paced its length.

"You're still really sore?" Quentin asked.

"There isn't a spot on my left side that doesn't ache."

"And you're upset. What's wrong?"

"What isn't? I thought by now we'd know so much, but the hypnosis was a waste of time. A purple snake, for the love of heaven!"

Quentin saw the barely leashed frustration that followed her dashed hopes. Sympathy filled him. "You're wrong. We know some important things we didn't know before."

"Such as?"

"First, we can be fairly certain that the motive behind the harassment is rooted in your past. More precisely, in something that happened on the night of the fire. Second, we know that you likely saw a man commit a criminal act serious enough for him to attempt to harm you back then and to try it again a couple of days ago."

Merrilee considered Quentin's claims for several seconds before she nodded in agreement. "But how do the snakes figure into this?"

"That I don't know yet, but let's discuss all this over something warm and sweet."

"Okay."

The session had taken a lot out of her. Maybe they shouldn't have held it so soon after the accident, but with each passing day her tormentor seemed to grow bolder or more desperate. Merrilee had been lucky so far, but luck wasn't anything Quentin liked to rely on. He needed facts, intuitive hunches, deductions—whatever he could get to stop the increasingly serious attacks on her.

"Where are we going?"

"McGuire's."

"The candy store?"

"In the back they serve the best hot-fudge sundaes I've ever eaten. Sound good?"

"Perfect."

They drove in silence to the candy store and tacitly postponed their serious discussion until they'd eaten the delicious concoction.

"Would you like another?" Quentin asked when he saw her scrape the last smidgen of chocolate from the bottom of the parfait glass.

Merrilee smiled. "No, thanks, I couldn't eat another one, but I want to finish this one down to the last bit of chocolate." She sighed contentedly. "That was perfect. Thank you."

She took a sip of water before she expressed the thought that had been circling in her brain. "I've been trying to come up with a list of crimes this man might have committed on the night of the fire. No matter how I turn it, it has to be something that's connected with my mother and the fire." When he didn't disagree, she added, "So, you've thought of that too."

"Yes. I've read the newspaper accounts of the fire, and I tried to get a hold of the official report, but it seems to have disappeared. According to the deputy who's been on the police force for many years, it might have been lost in the flood they had following a tornado. Of course, it also could have disappeared before then."

"Deliberately *made* to disappear?"

Quentin nodded.

"When I looked at old motor vehicle registrations, I was in a room in the courthouse basement that contained enormous filing cabinets. I wonder if the report could be in there."

"It's doubtful. If there was something questionable in the report, it likely would have been destroyed."

"How could he have gotten a hold of it?"

"Bribed someone. Or stole it."

"Are any of the officers who responded to the fire still around?"

"One is: Sheriff Chapman. At the time he was a deputy and involved in the investigation," Quentin told her.

"He's not the type to volunteer information or break down and confess if he did something wrong. Another dead end."

"Not necessarily. We'll have to attack the problem from the other end. From the victim's."

"My mother?"

"Are you willing to do that? You might find out some things you won't like."

"I know. Della already hinted that my mother might have been intimately involved with my father before they were married. Not that that bothers me," she added. "I'd like to know more about my mother. Even if it isn't all flattering. My life hasn't been perfect. I'm not in a position to judge her."

Quentin changed the subject. "I got a report back from the central crime lab on the body found in the cemetery. I sent the murdered man's fingerprints to them, and they identified them as belonging to one Ferlin Young."

"What? The same man who owned a Lincoln twenty-six years ago and lived in the same rooming house as my mother? He was spying on me?"

"Ferlin's an unusual-enough name that I'm willing to bet it's the same guy. The story of his identity is in today's *Evening Standard.* Maybe somebody will come forward with additional information on him or to claim the body."

"The crime lab only identified him? They had nothing else on him? Or is that confidential?"

"No. It's a matter of record. Seems Ferlin Young's been skirting the law for years. He's got an arrest record in the county. According to the deputy I usually deal with, he'd been pulled in for suspicion of bootlegging moonshine and later for trafficking in marijuana. Then there's a long time span when he either went straight or—"

"The sheriff's office looked the other way?"

"Not the entire office, but he might have enjoyed the protection of some members of the department." Quentin paused to sip some tea. "Six years ago he got picked up on a charge of drug dealing. He spent the last five years in prison."

"When he was paroled, he came straight back here?"

"Yes."

"Wouldn't he have needed a job, and wouldn't he have to report to a probation officer?"

Quentin nodded.

"Who gave him a job?"

"The Bufords. At their sawmill. More specifically, Deke Buford—Mrs. Buford's son and the heir apparent to the family fortune."

"Why would Deke Buford do that?"

"Possibly because he believes in the rehabilitation process, or maybe he's a kind man, though he doesn't strike me as one. Several times his lady friend arrived in the emergency room with suspicious-looking injuries."

Merrilee digested this information, trying to make sense of it. "What sort of job did Deke give Ferlin?"

"Something at their sawmill out in the county."

"Ferlin is part of all this, but since he's dead, he's not the one trying to kill me. I wish we knew what part he played in the harassment and why he was killed." Merrilee sighed. "And how does Bridie Cosgrove fit into all this? Snakes are involved, and she's apparently a master snake handler. And she knows my aunt."

"How long have you known her?"

"For as long as I can remember. Willadean used to drag me to their church and Sunday school. Bridie was the Sunday school teacher. She never liked me. And later, when I lived alone, she'd come to inspect the house. She always found something to criticize. She was a witch, but that hardly qualifies her as a potential killer. This is getting stranger and stranger."

"Cases often get stranger before they're solved."

"I think we should talk to Della Smith again. I know she was holding something back. Maybe if you came along, she'd be intimidated and tell all she knows."

Quentin glanced at his watch. "Okay, I'm game. Let's talk to both of them. Otis wasn't exactly open the last time we were there."

This time they found the Smiths' trailer without any difficulty. Otis invited them in but only reluctantly, his expression sullen. Though Quentin was used to people meeting him with a measure of wariness even when he was out of uniform, Otis' eyes were hostile, his body language guarded.

As soon as they were seated on the couch facing Otis in his rocking chair, Merrilee said, "Actually, we came to see Della."

Quentin saw Otis relax and reach for his whittling. He studied the piece of wood leisurely before he deigned to speak. "Well, I'm sorry to say that you made the long trip for nothin'. Della's visitin' her sister."

Otis's smug, sly expression irritated Quentin. "In that case we'll have to talk to you." He smiled rather wolfishly at Otis. Satisfied, he saw some of the older man's self-satisfied air disappear.

"I heard you were in a car accident," Otis said, looking at Merrilee. "You okay?"

Merrilee was clearly taken aback by Otis's comment. When she spoke, she couldn't hide the suspicion she felt. "I'm all right, thank you, but how did you know about my accident?"

"Della told me. She heard it at the Buford mansion. Miz Buford's on the hospital board, so any time somethin' interestin' happens, they telephone her." He stopped whittling and glowered at Merrilee. "The way you said that, makes a body think you suspected me or Della of having somethin' to do with your accident."

"What makes you think somebody had something to do with Miss Ingram's accident?" Quentin fixed Otis with a cool-eyed stare.

The question hit home, flustering the whittler into pausing. "The hospital switchboard operator told Miz Buford that Merrilee lost control of her car and ran off the road. In my experience, there's usually a reason for that kind of accident. Maybe another driver, or something in the road?"

"Have you read today's *Evening Standard*?" Quentin asked.

"Not yet. Is there something interesting in it?"

"I think so. We identified the murdered man we found in the cemetery. It's someone you knew—Ferlin Young."

The knife slipped and nicked Otis's finger. A drop of bright red blood domed up and then ran down the finger. Otis was too smart to try to cover up his telling reaction. He took his time wiping the blood onto his coveralls.

"Is that so?" he finally managed to ask. "Well, well. My ma used to say Ferlin wasn't fit to roll with a pig, but who'd have thought he'd get hisself murdered?"

"Any ideas on why he got himself killed or who might have done it?" Quentin asked.

Otis shook his head. "Lessen it was somebody he met in the penitentiary, I wouldn't have no idea. Folks around here liked him. Except Ma. But you can't accuse her, since she's been singin' with the heavenly choir for some time now." Otis grinned. "It must have been a robbery. Ferlin always carried cash and wore expensive clothes."

"Had you seen him since he was released from prison?" Quentin asked.

"I ain't seen Ferlin in years."

"Then how do you know he wore expensive clothes?" Quentin watched Otis closely.

"I know because Ferlin always dressed fit to kill."

"Where do you suppose he got the money for expensive clothes?"

Otis shrugged. "I don't rightly know. Ferlin always had money. I often wondered where he got it. Ma used to say he was like an old tick gettin' fat off a hard-working hound."

Quentin doubted that the source of Ferlin's illegal income was a secret to Otis but let that pass for the moment. "Where was he working thirty years ago?"

The question threw Otis. He took off his greasy cap and scratched the gray fringe around his bald pate. "That goes back a piece. At that time he must have been workin' for the Buford Bank. Yup. It surprised Ma considerable that Deke hired him on there and that his mammy allowed it."

"Why do you suppose Lurlene Buford allowed it?"

"That was during Deke's period of hell-raising. I

reckon Miz Buford thought giving one of his buddies a job might keep her boy from driving over to Sin City to visit the tattoo parlors and pleasure palaces."

"Sin City?" Merrilee asked.

"Memphis."

"Did it work?"

"Not so much."

"Where were you working at the time?" Quentin asked.

"At the bank too. They wasn't hirin' at the mill or the mines. I was lucky to get work on the bank's night cleaning crew."

"Did Ferlin work with you?" Merrilee asked.

Otis hooted with laughter. "Shoot, no. Ferlin wouldn't have been caught dead pushin' a broom. Too good for such low work. He was a security guard."

"My mother worked at the bank too. Is that where you met her?"

"Naw. I met her right after she moved to town and took a room at Miller's boarding house. I lived there for a spell too before Della and me got hitched."

"Then you all must have known each other well, you and Ferlin and my mother, since you lived and worked in the same place. Did she date Ferlin?"

"Reba was the best-lookin' woman in these parts. She wouldn't have wasted her time on Ferlin."

"Whom did she date before she married my dad? Deke Buford?"

Briefly an odd expression flitted across Otis' face. Then he concentrated on his whittling for a few seconds before he spoke. "Well, Deke surely tried. He was always sniffin' around Reba, but she looked at him like somethin' she wanted to step on. I don't recall who she saw before she married Rafe."

Quentin glanced at Merrilee, wondering if she'd caught the lie. Otis struck him as a man who'd always make sure he knew everything about everybody.

"Mr. Smith, are you sure you don't want to rephrase your answer about not having seen Ferlin since his release?"

"You going to ask me that question at the jailhouse?"

"I might."

"Well, I might have seen him around town."

"Is that when you noticed his expensive clothes?"

"Yup."

"Didn't you wonder how he could afford them right out of prison and working as a laborer at the sawmill?"

"As a laborer?" Otis looked as if he couldn't have heard what he'd heard. "Ferlin never worked a day in his life as a laborer. Hated to get his lily-white hands dirty. Maybe on the payroll he was listed as a laborer, but I'm willin' to bet my best coon dog that he didn't 'labor' on the floor of the mill."

"What hold did he have on Deke Buford to get a job right out of prison?" The question clearly made Otis uncomfortable, maybe even afraid. He didn't even pretend an interest in his whittling.

"Ferlin didn't have nothin' on Deke. Who said he did?" Otis demanded, his tone blustering.

"Just something I heard around town," Quentin said.

"Chief, surely a man in your position don't listen to gossip."

Quentin studied his fingernails. Blandly he said, "You know the old saying about where there's smoke, there's fire."

"Them old sayings don't mean nothin'," Otis said. "Deke is one of the most respectable businessmen in town."

Quentin didn't bother to acknowledge that remark. Instead he rose. "If you think of something concerning Ferlin Young that you forgot to mention, call me."

As soon as they were out of earshot, Merrilee asked, "Did you really hear such a rumor?"

"No, but it was a logical assumption based on my reading of Deke Buford's character. I doubt that he would do anything for anyone out of mere friendship. Therefore, Ferlin must have had something on him."

"Which makes Deke a candidate for being a murderer, doesn't it?"

"Yes, but he's got an alibi for the time of Ferlin's death. He was at the state capital, attending a fundraiser for his brother-in-law, Earl Mainwright."

"But he could have hired somebody to do it or ducked out early. It's not that long a drive."

"That's true," Quentin conceded.

"How did you know that Otis knew Ferlin?"

"An educated guess. They're both roughly the same age and from around here. It would be highly improbable that they hadn't known each other. I had no idea, though, that they'd lived in the same rooming house and worked in the same place."

Merrilee thought about that all the way back to Oak Street. "Did you think Otis' loyal defense of Deke Buford rang true?"

"There was a good deal of self-interest in his defense. Makes me wonder what Otis owes Deke."

Merrilee shut off the alarm system. Quentin followed her into the house.

"You want to get a few overnight things together?"

"No. I've changed my mind. I'm staying here." When Quentin looked as if he were about to launch into a protest, she explained. "This is my home. I refuse to be continuously driven from it. I've just had an excellent security system installed. I also have the gun Howard gave me. And if I have bad dreams, I'll have them at the Farmers' the same as here.

Quentin admired her determination. Before he could say anything, the phone shrilled. Merrilee answered it.

"It's for you," she said, holding the receiver out to him.

When the dispatcher gave him the message, Quentin's heart ached for Merrilee.

"Merrilee, that call was about your aunt."

Something in his voice caused her to tremble. "She's had a heart attack?" she whispered.

"I'm afraid it's worse than that. I'm sorry."

Chapter Fourteen

Quentin wished Merrilee would break down and cry. Like most men, he felt acutely uncomfortable in the presence of women's tears, but this was one time when he would have welcomed them. For the past two days he had watched her hold herself together by sheer willpower alone.

Stoically she had made arrangements with the funeral parlor, firmly refusing John Cosgrove's offer to conduct the service. Dry-eyed she had allowed Peggy to fuss over her without complaining. Merrilee spoke little, ate less, and didn't sleep at all. She had pulled her grief around her like a cloak, permitting no one and nothing to penetrate it.

They sat side by side on the living room sofa, waiting for Dr. Albright, who had requested this joint meeting.

After a lengthy silence she asked, "Did the doctor

say why he wants to see us? He already expressed his condolences."

"He didn't say." When the doorbell rang, Quentin answered it. Surprised, he saw that Dr. Albright was accompanied by Sam Stewart, the attorney. Though their expressions were guarded, Quentin knew something was wrong.

After greetings were exchanged and everyone was seated, Dr. Albright said, "Miss Ingram, you look as if you haven't slept for days. I brought you a mild sedative. Take it tonight."

She accepted the small envelope containing a single pill. It was the same kind her aunt had taken. "Thank you."

The doctor cleared his throat a couple of times before he spoke. "There's no easy way to say this, so I won't beat around the bush. Miss Ingram, I want your permission to have an autopsy performed on your aunt."

Merrilee gasped as the realization of what an autopsy meant hit her. "No," she whispered.

"Merrilee, the doctor wouldn't make this request if he didn't have a pressing reason," Quentin pointed out. "Please hear him out."

"What reason? Dr. Albright, what happened?"

"That's what we want to find out."

"We? You and Mr. Stewart?"

"And Dr. Maddox. He's the physician who covered for me while I was on vacation."

Merrilee looked bewildered. "What do you think happened?"

"It's more what I and Dr. Maddox don't think should have happened."

An evasive answer to pacify Merrilee, except it wasn't going to work. In order to save time, Quentin intervened. "That doesn't explain Mr. Stewart's presence. Unless you brought him along because you fear a lawsuit?"

"No. I don't think there are grounds for litigation. Mr. Stewart called me to ask . . . Why don't you explain, Sam?"

"Gladly. Did your aunt talk to you about her will?"

"No."

"About money?"

"Not exactly, but when I said I wanted to put her into a private room and pay for the difference in cost, she said she had money."

"Would it surprise you to learn that she wanted to change her will and make you her beneficiary?"

Merrilee's throat tightened painfully with suppressed tears, preventing her from speaking for several seconds. Finally she managed to choke out an answer. "She knew I didn't really need money, but because we were family, she might have felt it proper to pass her possessions on to me."

"Do you know who her beneficiaries were?"

Merrilee shook her head.

"John Cosgrove and his church."

Quentin saw that that surprised and shocked her. He couldn't blame her. He watched her struggle with her feelings.

"It makes sense for my aunt to leave her money to a religious organization, but I truly wish it hadn't been Cosgrove's congregation."

"Have you any idea of the sum involved?"

"Mr. Stewart, my aunt was a missionary all her life. They're not exactly in a high-income bracket."

"No, but it seems her husband had a shrewd sense of money. He lent her earnings to the poor people they worked with at hefty interest rates."

Merrilee looked stunned. "Poor Aunt Hazel. How she would have hated that. No wonder she felt so betrayed by her husband. When did she find this out?"

"Apparently not until after his death. She felt guilty and embarrassed when she told me about it."

Merrilee nodded. "Her guilt ran deep. She wanted to atone for it even though she personally hadn't done anything wrong."

"Mr. Stewart, how much money is involved in Mrs. Peterson's estate?" Quentin asked.

"About a million dollars."

An astonished hush fell over the room. Recovering from her amazement at the figure, Merrilee asked, "Are you sure?"

"Positive. I've been handling your aunt's affairs since she returned to this country. Seems her husband wanted Brother John to inherit. Your aunt hadn't quite brought herself to go against his wishes until she met you."

Quentin now realized where all this was heading. His heart filled with compassion for Merrilee. "Dr. Albright, do you have reasonable medical grounds for your suspicions?"

"Yes, I do."

Merrilee looked searchingly at each man's face. "What grounds? What's going on? Will someone please tell me?"

Quentin heard the note of panic in her voice. He reached out to place a hand comfortingly on her shoulder.

Facing Quentin, her voice full of despair, she asked, "What's going on? Aunt Hazel just died, and now there's to be an autopsy because . . . Why exactly, Dr. Albright?"

"I think we'd better tell Miss Ingram the truth," Sam Stewart said. When the doctor nodded, the attorney said, "When I heard that Mrs. Peterson passed away unexpectedly shortly after we discussed changing her beneficiary, I naturally telephoned her physician to confirm that everything was aboveboard."

"Aboveboard? What does that mean?" Merrilee demanded.

"That your aunt died of natural causes."

Merrilee gasped. "Oh, my God."

Her lips were bloodless, her eyes horrified. Quentin moved closer to her on the sofa. He wasn't sure how she would react when the full implication hit her. He watched her take a couple of breaths, trying to remain calm, but they were shallow breaths, indicating the depth of her anxiety.

"Are you trying to tell me that my aunt . . . that someone . . ." Merrilee was unable to finish the sentence.

"We're not sure. Not without an autopsy," the doctor said.

"But something leads you to suspect foul play?" Quentin asked.

"Yes."

"What?" Merrilee demanded. "Aunt Hazel had a weak heart. I thought that was the cause of death."

"It was. What we want to know is exactly what triggered the serious arrhythmia."

"An autopsy will show that?"

"Yes. It'll tell us how much digitalis was in her body."

"I thought digitalis was one of her daily medications."

"It was, but if too much is given, digitalis intoxication or poisoning occurs, and the resulting ventricular fibrillation causes death."

"You think someone at the nursing home made a mistake in Aunt Hazel's dosage?" Merrilee asked.

"Maybe, but it's highly unlikely. The dosage's been the same for a while. Nor has the staff changed, so the same nurses have been taking care of your aunt. Gladys Vernon may have an abrasive personality at times, but she runs a tight ship."

"If the overdose wasn't accidental . . ." Merrilee's voice trailed off.

"We can't know anything for sure until after an autopsy," Dr. Albright stated. "Will you give permission for us to perform it?"

"Yes."

The doctor placed a document and a pen on the coffee table in front of Merrilee.

She read it and then signed it. "How soon will you know the results?"

"In a couple of days."

"In the meantime, no one but us should know about this," Quentin said.

They all agreed.

"We'll go so you can get some rest. Don't forget to take the pill," Dr. Albright urged.

"I won't forget."

Quentin accompanied the men to the door. Then he went into the kitchen. When he rejoined Merrilee, he carried a large glass of orange juice. "Drink," he said. "When the body is under a lot of stress, it needs extra vitamin C."

She took the glass and drank some of the juice. "I feel as if I stepped through some crazy mirror into a world where nothing is right anymore. Aunt Hazel's gone. Since we just found each other after all these years, it's so hard to accept." Her voice broke. When she could, she said, "Now Dr. Albright says that maybe it wasn't God who took her life but someone else."

Merrilee pressed her hands over her eyes. Suddenly rough, choking sounds escaped her throat. She rocked back and forth. Her grief erupted in keening sounds that tore at Quentin.

Gently he lowered her hands from her face and wrapped his arms around her. "It's okay to cry. Your aunt deserves some tears." Merrilee collapsed against him. It seemed to Quentin that she wept like someone who had previously forgotten how—her pain poured out in hot tears accompanied by harsh, hoarse sobs that racked her body. She cried for a long time.

"I'm sorry. For a woman who never cries, I sure am making up for lost time."

"It's all right."

"I didn't know tears took that much out of a person." Merrilee wiped her face with the back of her left hand.

Quentin studied her face. She looked exhausted, but that stony, stoic expression was gone. "Hold out your hand." Quentin shook the sleeping pill into her palm. When she placed it into her mouth, he handed her the remaining juice.

"The pill will guarantee you at least eight hours of undisturbed sleep, which you need. Come, I'll walk you upstairs and tuck you in."

She didn't object and went with him obediently. He waited in the hall outside her bedroom until she called him. When Quentin saw her standing in the middle of the room, his breath caught. In her white satin pajamas trimmed with tiny pearl buttons, she looked like a woman straight out of a romantic film made during Hollywood's heyday. Reminding himself how exhausted, how vulnerable she was, he forced himself to walk past her, remove the bedspread, and turn the quilt back for her. After she slipped into bed, he tucked the cover around her.

"Will you stay until I fall asleep?"

"Yes." Quentin moved the chair from the dressing table next to the bed.

"Thanks," she murmured, flashing him a small, wan smile. Then she sighed deeply and closed her eyes.

She was probably asleep within seconds, but he stayed for a while longer, watching over her.

Two days later, under a lowering sky hung with clouds almost the color of the mud-gray wet earth flanking the open grave, they laid Hazel Jones Peterson to rest.

Merrilee insisted on the old-fashioned service, convinced that her aunt would have preferred that. Instinctively Merrilee knew she had to face her loss head-on. She could not walk away from a flower-covered casket sitting prettily among the wreaths and pretend that that was all there was to death. She needed to see the coffin lowered into the cold earth, needed to murmur "ashes to ashes, dust to dust," needed to taste the full bitterness of her loss before she could come to terms with it and eventually accept and endure it.

Over Merrilee's protests, Peggy had insisted on hosting a reception after the funeral, arguing that this was the customary thing to do. If Merrilee didn't allow it, the Farmers could never hold up their heads in the community again. In the end it had been easier to give in, especially since all Merrilee had to do was pay for the food and drink and greet the people as they arrived. Peggy arranged everything else.

Now, forty-eight hours later, Merrilee was waiting for Quentin. From his voice over the telephone she guessed he had news. To help remain composed until his arrival, Merrilee sat at the piano, working on the song she was writing in memory of her aunt. She had the tune pretty well worked out, but the words to fit the plaintive yet celebratory melody wouldn't come.

"That's a lovely melody," Quentin said when Merrilee answered the doorbell. "I must confess I've been standing on the porch, listening to you for a couple of minutes."

"In this cold? Come in." Shivering, she shut the door behind him quickly. "Let me take your coat."

"It's a nasty night out there," he said, handing her the coat.

"Would you like some hot tea?"

"I'd love a cup."

Merrilee led the way to the kitchen, where she busied herself preparing a pot of tea. Her hands shook.

She tried to steel herself, to hide the turmoil that rioted in her heart. "There's some of Peggy's lemon pound cake left. Would you like some?" she asked, her voice shaky.

"Sure. I never turn down any of Peggy's baking."

Merrilee felt Quentin's eyes watching her the whole time. His stance only added to her anxiety.

"Is that melody you played part of a new song?" Quentin accepted a cup of tea with a smile.

"Yes. It's . . . it's in memory of Aunt Hazel." She lowered her gaze to hide the moisture pooling there. She should never have given in to tears in the first place. Now every time she turned around, she felt like crying.

Quentin ate the cake, watching her struggle valiantly against tears. After a lengthy silence he felt compelled to say, "It's okay to cry again. Nobody is keeping score."

"It's weak and foolish and useless."

"It's also human." Quentin reached across the table and laid his hand on hers. She wouldn't or couldn't look at him. He gave her time to compose herself. When her fingers stopped trembling, he said quietly, "I have some information." She raised her gaze to his. He saw fear in her eyes, but also determination to face what he had to say.

"I thought you might have. Tell me, please."

"The autopsy showed a quantity of digitalis in your aunt's body far in excess of the prescribed dosage."

"Which means she was poisoned," Merrilee whispered, and she walked to the sink. Grasping its edge to steady herself, she closed her eyes in agony. "Aunt Hazel didn't have to die. Somebody took her life willfully and wantonly. Who could have been so hateful?"

He watched her raise her hands to her face, whether to try to stop the tears or to hide them, Quentin couldn't tell. Tenderly he turned her body to face his, placed his arms around her, and let her weep. He felt anger stiffen her even before the last of her tears subsided.

"Who?" she demanded, looking at him with tear-washed eyes. "Who did this to her?"

"I don't know. Yet. But I will. You can count on that."

"I want him punished. I want him drawn and quartered, or hanged or decapitated or whatever is the most painful." When she realized what she'd said, she shook her head. "I didn't know I could feel such anger, such a lust for raw vengeance."

"That's not unnatural."

She took a ragged breath. "I want to find out who did this to Aunt Hazel."

"You can help," he said, and he led her back to the table. He refilled her cup. "Think back carefully. You may have noticed something at the nursing home that seemed insignificant at the time."

Merrilee dabbed her wet face with a paper napkin from the holder on the table. "Where do we start? With the motive?"

"Knowing the motive definitely helps in solving a case. Usually I ask who had the opportunity and the means and who profited by the victim's death."

Merrilee blanched. "The next of kin, right?"

He nodded. "Except in your case. Even though your aunt spoke of changing her will, she hadn't gotten around to it. She left everything to John Cosgrove and his church."

Merrilee brooded for several seconds before she spoke. "No matter how much I dislike John Cosgrove, I can't imagine him committing murder. A lot of other things, but not murder. He may be narrow-minded in his beliefs, but they're strong and sincere. Almost fanatical. I can't see him in the role of murderer."

"I checked the financial resources of his church. They're not good. In order to save the church, he might have felt justified in committing murder. But I agree with you that that is unlikely. He's not a strong suspect. And he has an ironclad alibi. During the crucial time he was conducting a revival meeting in a tent pitched next to the Wallace grocery store in Mt. Hebron."

"We're back to Mt. Hebron," Merrilee murmured thoughtfully.

"When I drove over there, Mr. Wallace wasn't home. I want to talk to him again. He's an observant man. If anything out of the ordinary happened at the revival, he will have noticed. I also want to confirm that Bridie Cosgrove is Sula Jennings' daughter."

"At first I couldn't reconcile the meek, mealy-mouthed, washed-out looking Bridie with the image of a snake handler, but the more I thought about it, the more conceivable it became. There is a cruel streak in her that Mr. Wallace noticed too. In Sunday school she used to pinch the children who didn't behave," Merrilee said.

"I haven't been able to pinpoint Mrs. Cosgrove's whereabouts for every hour of the revival. She was there, but John was the star. People remember seeing Bridie, but no one can vouch for her being there the whole time."

"She might have had an opportunity to slip away, but what about motive? The will doesn't mention her."

"True, but she gains indirectly through her husband," Quentin pointed out.

"Did you ask Mr. Stewart just how the money is to be given to the church? Does John make the decisions on how it's spent?"

"Yeah, I asked him. Sam said that half of it is to be used for the church, and half is to be invested to provide a retirement fund for John as well as pay for a comprehensive health insurance policy. So he actually doesn't get his hands on a lump sum, but, as Sam pointed out, he could interpret spending the church's half in all sorts of creative ways to benefit himself."

"So they have motive. And even though I asked that they not be admitted to my aunt's room, security at the nursing home is lax at best. I have walked in when no one was at the front desk. The Cosgroves could have sneaked in quite easily. But what about the digitalis? It's not exactly an over-the-counter medication."

"That had me stumped for a while until Dr. Albright mentioned that digitalis is made from the foxglove plant. In the old days physicians administered it brewed as a tea. You can find foxglove in many local gardens."

Merrilee drew in her breath sharply. "It's that simple?"

"Apparently. Dr. Albright is waiting for the results of a more sophisticated test to find out in what form it was administered."

Merrilee thought this over for a while. Finally she shook her head. "But why? I can't imagine Aunt Hazel's ever having hurt anyone. And I would have talked her out of changing her will."

"But nobody knew that."

"So to some degree I contributed to her death."

"Merrilee, that's ridiculous. Don't you dare think that." To distract her, he said, "I've talked to Deke Buford about employing Ferlin Young. He claims he did it out of loyalty to their old friendship and that he has no ideas at all about Ferlin's murder. He thinks it must have been someone Ferlin met in prison."

"That's what Otis claimed too."

Quentin nodded. "Both are lying. Both are hiding

something. I have a hunch it's something that goes back to their younger years."

"Speaking of the Bufords, the queen bee herself phoned me. After extending her condolences, she badgered me into attending a fund-raising party to restore the Watkins House. That woman's like a steamroller. She claims that throwing myself into the Watkins House project will honor my aunt more than grieving by myself."

"For once I'm glad she's so persistent. It'll be good for you to get out of the house. When will you meet with Dr. Harrison again?"

"On Wednesday."

"Are you worried about it?"

Merrilee considered the question. "Not nearly as much as I was. Now I want to know once and for all what happened. I want to face the past and put it behind me, where it belongs."

"That's what I've been waiting to hear."

Merrilee noticed Quentin's warm smile. For the first time in days she felt a little more cheerful.

"Can you be ready to drive to Mt. Hebron with me after supper?"

"Yes." Merrilee found herself looking forward to the trip.

Chapter Fifteen

Despite the pep talk she'd given herself, Merrilee sat for several minutes in the car before she worked up her courage to walk into the nursing home. After that first trip to the home, she had looked forward to her visits with her aunt, of whom she'd become genuinely fond. Now she was gone forever.

Ethel Mae was sitting propped up in bed, watching a game show, which she switched off the moment she saw Merrilee.

"I'm so sorry about Hazel. They wouldn't let me go to the funeral because I was just getting over a bad chest cold. It's a sorry state when a body can't even pay her last respects."

"I'm sure Aunt Hazel understood why you weren't there."

Ethel Mae nodded. "She was a wise and understanding woman, Hazel was. I'll miss her. I'm gettin' a new roommate. Bet she ain't as nice as Hazel was. You come to fetch her things?"

"Yes."

"Good. Them two pushy Bible-thumpers have been around, but I told them to leave Hazel's personal things alone. I can't believe they'll get her money. I know she meant for you to inherit. She told me so. Said she was feelin' better after she talked to the lawyer and was fixing to leave everything to you, her blood kin. That's as it should be. You should hire a smart lawyer and fight for what's yours."

"I'll think about it," Merrilee said to quiet Ethel Mae, who'd become agitated. She had no intention of taking the Cosgroves to court. Merrilee emptied Hazel's few toiletries into a paper sack. Her hands shook when she touched the brush she had used on her aunt's hair. When she saw the pink quilted robe she'd bought for Hazel, she felt tears fill her eyes.

Ethel Mae looked at the robe. "That's the prettiest robe I ever saw. Hazel purely loved it."

Noting the woman's shapeless housecoat that reminded Merrilee of a horse blanket, she asked, "Would you like the robe? I'm sure Hazel would approve of your having it."

"Really?"

"Of course." Merrilee took the robe and held it for Ethel Mae, who'd quickly slipped out of bed and discarded her old robe.

After she buttoned it, she ran her hands reverently

over the satiny material. "I ain't never owned nothing this nice. My husband got killed in the mine, so I had all them kids to raise by myself."

"Well, wear it in good health and in memory of Hazel."

"I will."

"Ethel Mae, when was the last time you saw the Cosgroves here?"

"Yesterday. I told you they came sniffing around."

"And before that?"

"Well, I didn't actually see them, but I know they was here. At least the woman was. Let me see . . . must have been the day your aunt died."

Merrilee caught her breath. "Are you sure?"

"I'm sure."

"If you didn't see her, how can you be sure Bridie Cosgrove was here?"

"By the smell."

Merrilee felt keenly disappointed. Apparently Ethel Mae had mistaken someone else for Bridie. Though the preacher's wife was no fashion plate, she didn't smell.

"I'd know the smell of that tonic anywhere." Ethel Mae grimaced as if she'd bitten into a lemon. "That tonic not only smelled bad, it tasted worse. I don't know how your aunt could drink it without gagging. I can't abide sassafras or licorice."

Now Merrilee understood. "When did Bridie bring a tonic?"

"First time was a week before Hazel passed away. Badgered your poor aunt into drinking it."

"And you smelled the tonic again the day my aunt died?"

"Sure did. Bridie must have snuck in when I was in the dispensary, gettin' my vitamin shot. I was going to tease Hazel about the tonic, but she was asleep when I came back to the room. Then they came to take me to the hospital. When I got back the next morning, Hazel was gone. Never even had a chance to say good-bye."

"Did you see what Bridie brought the tonic in?"

"Yeah. Looked like a vinegar bottle to me."

"How big was it?"

"Pint-sized, I'd say."

"Thanks, Ethel Mae. That's a big help."

Merrilee rushed out of the room. She questioned Gladys about the bottle.

"We probably still have it. We recycle everything. We place all glass items in a bin out back. I can get our custodian to look through it when he comes tonight."

"I can't wait that long. May I look through the bin?"

Gladys looked surprised but agreed.

By the time she found the vinegar bottle, Merrilee was convinced that she had rooted through glass jars and bottles of all sizes known to God and man. She unscrewed the top and took a cautious sniff. Hallelujah! The scent of sassafras and licorice was unmistakable. There was even a little bit of dark liquid left in the bottle. Though she couldn't be certain, it seemed to be enough for a lab analysis. She could hardly wait to see Quentin's face when she handed her discovery to him.

In that she was to be disappointed. Bob Lee informed her that Quentin was out on a call when she arrived at the station. She wrote a note explaining the circumstances of her discovery and left it with the bottle on Quentin's desk. Then she hurried home to get ready for the Buford fund-raising party.

Three hours later Merrilee double-checked the address Lurlene Buford had given her. Either she had copied it down wrong or the Watkins House party was scheduled to take place at Earl Mainwright's storefront election headquarters. Surely that couldn't be. The lieutenant governor struck her as a man who wouldn't stoop so low as to use an event sponsored by the historical society to get a little extra publicity. His mother-in-law, on the other hand, probably would.

Merrilee paused to study a poster of the candidate. Earl Mainwright was still a handsome man, tall without any extra weight on his body, his eyes a clear, bright blue, his wavy, reddish hair silver-streaked. As an entertainer, Merrilee knew all about the importance of a winning appearance. Whoever had worked on the candidate's image had done a good job. Studying his face, she noted the native intelligence and humor in the blue eyes. Those were qualities no image maker could create.

"Merrilee Ingram? It *is* you. Well, I declare."

Merrilee looked at the young woman bearing down on her with a welcoming smile on her pretty face. Someone she should remember, and though the woman's features were familiar, Merrilee couldn't put a name to them.

"I'm Naomi Kincaid." The smile wavered a little, then recovered. "Well, you knew me as Naomi Price."

"Yes, of course. You lived near Miss Willadean's. How are you?"

"Good. Are you coming to the Watkins House shindig?"

"If I ever find it." Merrilee glanced at the number over the seemingly locked door to the headquarters' entrance.

Naomi laughed. "I guess to someone who doesn't live here, the address could cause confusion. The party's upstairs. The Bufords own the building, so Lurlene gave the historical society the use of the upstairs for free. I'm sure it's a tax write-off," Naomi confided in a stage whisper. "Come, I'll go up with you." She led the way to a small door set inconspicuously between the display windows of the storefront.

"I don't know if you remember, but this used to be the Perkins' furniture store." Without waiting, Naomi chattered on. "You're probably wondering how someone like me ended up doing volunteer work for the historical society."

Merrilee, who hadn't wondered anything of the sort, uttered a noncommittal sound.

"Well, I'm divorced, and Browne's Station isn't exactly jumping with possibilities to cut loose. Not that the historical society is all that exciting, but it beats sitting home night after night. But then, the kind of life you lead, you wouldn't know about that."

Merrilee was about to reply that she didn't know

much about sitting at home since roughly two-thirds of her evenings were spent working or sitting on the group's bus traveling to the next gig, when they reached the top of the stairs and the noisy open space beyond.

"Let's take our coats off," Naomi suggested. They did.

"We'd better go say hi to Mrs. Buford and Miss Pet before we get our refreshments."

Naomi started to steer Merrilee through the crowd toward the other side of the room, but their progress was impeded by a number of women thrusting their small cocktail napkins at Merrilee for her autograph. She obliged with a smile and a few friendly words.

"Are you always so obliging about giving autographs?" Lurlene asked, fingering the heavy pearl and diamond choker straining around her thick neck.

"Being nice to the public is part of being a performer."

"Part of politics too. Earl's always out shaking hands and talking to folks. Me, I couldn't do it. Guess it takes a special kind of person." Lurlene picked up the coffee cup sitting on the table next to her and took a sip. "I'm sorry about your aunt. Did she have kids of her own?"

"No."

"Children can be a real comfort and a real trial. Especially when they're teenagers. I recollect when my boy Deke was around seventeen. He came back from Memphis one time with the most awful tattoo on his arm. He's worn long-sleeved shirts ever since then when he's not wearing a jacket."

Lurlene shook her head. Not a single newly-dyed, hair-spray–stiff, jet-black hair moved. "Now that your aunt is gone, will you be going back to Nashville?"

Although Lurlene's little-girl voice was perfectly controlled, Merrilee knew that this was the question all the previous social chitchat had been leading up to. "I'm going to stay in Browne's Station for a while."

"What on earth for? It's not as if this were your home anymore or that you had kin here. Take my advice: you'd be much happier in Nashville."

Ordinarily a threat uttered in a squeaky, girlish voice would have struck Merrilee as ludicrous, but one look into the small black eyes filled with blatant hatred convinced Merrilee that she ought not to dismiss Lurlene's words lightly.

Apparently realizing that she had revealed her true feelings, Lurlene lowered her eyes. When she looked up, her face was a mask of social propriety. "On the other hand, our little town is a nice place to stay for a while," Lurlene said.

"Yes, it is. Excuse me," Merrilee said, making space for a newly arrived group of women. She walked toward the back of the hall, where she'd noticed the ladies' room. The encounter with Lurlene had left her more shaken than she'd like to admit. It was unnerving to be hated by someone without knowing the reason for the enmity.

In the powder room Merrilee searched her small

beaded bag in the hope that it might contain her small pillbox filled with aspirin. It didn't. Snapping the clasp shut, she glanced into the mirror, which revealed one corner of the partitioned-off section containing two stalls and a washbasin.

With her profile to Merrilee a woman stood in front of the basin, uncapped one of those miniature liquor bottles, raised it to her mouth, and didn't lower it until the bottle was empty.

Feeling like a voyeur even though she had not set out to spy, Merrilee moved to the right until she could no longer see the woman. She did so just in time to avoid being caught watching. The clicking of the woman's heels on the tile floor announced her approach. When their eyes met in the mirror, Merrilee couldn't tell which one of them was more surprised: she or Pet Mainwright.

The politician's wife paled. Under the bright fluorescent lighting Pet looked haggard. Part of that was undoubtedly due to the unflattering color of her dress; part of her pallor was probably due to the fear of discovery. To reassure the woman, Merrilee brushed her hair with unhurried strokes.

"How are you, Mrs. Mainwright?"

Merrilee's poise seemed to convince Petulia that her secret drinking was still a secret.

"I'm okay now, though I must confess I thought you were Reba when I first saw your face. Gave me quite a turn."

Merrilee stared at the woman. "I didn't realize you knew my Mom."

"Oh, we weren't friends or anything like that. After all, she was only hired help in the family bank."

"Did you work in the bank too?"

Pet removed the cigarette from her mouth and burst into high-pitched laughter. "Honey, my daddy *owned* the bank. I didn't work there. Earl did, way back then."

Sensing that the laughter was aimed at her mother, Merrilee couldn't resist a small jibe. "How convenient for you that your daddy owned the bank."

"What?" Two bright red spots appeared on Pet's gaunt cheeks. Her small black eyes glittered. Stabbing her cigarette in Merrilee's direction, she said, "Let me set you straight on something right now, Miss Song-bird. Earl loved me. He didn't marry me because I was the boss' daughter. Whoever says that is a bald-faced liar!"

The vehement outburst left Merrilee speechless. All she could do was watch the woman in the mirror. Pet's hand shook as she raised the cigarette to her mouth. Her body swayed slightly, suggesting that this wasn't her first trip to the bathroom for liquid refreshment.

"What are you staring at? So maybe I wasn't as good-looking as popular, pretty, precious Reba Jones, but Earl married *me*. And that's what counts. And we have a daughter, so he doesn't need another one."

What was the woman talking about? The alcohol must have muddled her brain. But whether Petulia was drunk or not, Merrilee wouldn't allow her mother to be disparaged. She squared her shoulders. "I'm sure it didn't hurt that your father was Earl's employer. The *only* employer in this one-horse town."

Merrilee watched Pet's eyes narrow into dangerous slits and her hand rise as if to strike her. "Don't even think of raising a hand against me. I have way more experience in fighting down and dirty than you have."

Pet stepped back. She dropped the cigarette she'd been holding and crushed it viciously under one shoe.

"Let me give you a piece of advice, Miss Reba's daughter. Get out of Browne's Station, and leave us alone. The sooner the better, if you know what's good for you." Pet turned and, holding herself with the careful rigidity of someone a little drunk, she stalked out of the powder room.

More than ever Merrilee felt the need for a couple of aspirin. Maybe Naomi had some. Better yet, she would go home for them. She obviously wasn't wanted here. Why on earth had Lurlene practically twisted her arm to get her to come here in the first place? To warn her? To tell her to get out of town? But why? None of this made any sense.

Returning to the main room, Merrilee skirted its edges toward the exit. She hadn't gone very far when a heavy, masculine hand gripped her shoulder to stop her.

"Hey, sugar, what are you doing here? I didn't think you were coming to this party."

Merrilee whirled around. If she'd had live snakes in her hair, the middle-aged man facing her couldn't have looked more shocked. The blood drained from his face, only to rush back and tint it beet-red. He snatched his hand from Merrilee's shoulder as if he'd touched a live wire.

"Excuse me," he muttered, still staring at her. "I thought you were Crystal. Your hair . . ." His voice trailed off. He turned sharply and hurried toward the back of the room as if the devil himself were pursuing him.

Merrilee stood there until Naomi joined her. "Is anything wrong? You look puzzled."

"That man back there," Merrilee said, pointing discreetly at the hastily retreating figure. "He thought I was Crystal. Who is he?"

"Deke Buford." Naomi studied Merrilee's hair. "You know, you and his niece have the same kind of red hair, so it's not so strange that he thought you were she."

"Naomi, I know some sort of program is scheduled after the reception, but I don't feel very well. Could you let me know later whatever it is I'm to contribute to this restoration effort? I have to go home and lie down."

"I understand. What with your aunt passing away, I can see where you aren't up to this. I'll get the information to you."

"Thanks a million." Merrilee smiled gratefully and escaped before anyone else could tell her to leave town or mistake her for someone else.

"Guess who I met yesterday," Naomi said, handing Quentin the time cards to sign.

"I couldn't possibly guess, but I assume it wasn't Elvis."

"Be serious, Chief."

Seeing her eager expression, he played along. "All right. Whom did you meet?"

"Merrilee Ingram. And she's real nice. Not a bit conceited. Remembered me right off the bat."

"Where did you meet her?"

"At the historical society reception for the Watkins House project. Mrs. Buford invited her. And Deke Buford mistook Merrilee for his niece, Crystal."

Quentin frowned. "What made him do that?"

"You've never met Crystal Mainwright, have you?"

"I don't think so."

"That explains it. It didn't strike me at first either, but the two women have the same red hair."

"What's so unusual about that? Lots of women have red hair."

"Not that shade of red. Not with the same thick texture and natural waviness." Naomi squinted at the wall, deep in thought. "You know what? They look alike in their features too. You don't notice it at first because Crystal's eyes are dark, like her mom's and her grandma's, and Merrilee's are bright blue, but aside from that and the fact that Merrilee is prettier, they look alike enough to be related. Isn't that odd?"

"Well, they say we each have a double somewhere." Quentin handed the signed cards back to Naomi. "Let me know the minute the lab results on that tonic are delivered."

Disappointed that Quentin wasn't intrigued by the coincidence of the red hair, Naomi muttered, "Men," and shook her head.

A knock on the door caused both of them to turn and look.

"May I come in?"

"We were just talking about you," Naomi said with a smile.

"Really?"

"About us meeting at the historical society reception. Are you feeling better?"

"Yes, thank you. What happened after I left?"

"Not much, other than Mrs. Buford's twisting everyone's arm to contribute generously. She'll be sending out letters suggesting the amount she thinks people should give."

"That's a little high-handed, isn't it?" Merrilee said.

"Not for Mrs. Buford. Excuse me, I have to take these to the accountant."

After Naomi left, Quentin asked Merrilee to sit down. "I heard Deke Buford mistook you for his niece."

"Yes, and his mother hinted that I'd find Browne's Station boring, and his sister told me to get out. And she also said something really odd about her husband's not needing another daughter." Merrilee frowned. "She'd been drinking, so that could explain her odd words. Still, I wish I knew why those women dislike me." Then, dismissing them, she added, "I have news."

"Yeah?"

"But it's not good news. After my run-in with the Bufords yesterday, I decided to get the truth out of Della once and for all, but the Smiths were gone."

"What?"

"They're gone. Otis and Della. Disappeared. Left. Moved. I drove out to their trailer. The first thing I noticed was the absence of all those dogs. And all the carvings were gone from the porch."

"Maybe Otis took them to some store to be sold to tourists."

"That's what I thought too until I looked through the windows. The place was completely empty."

"Maybe they went for a long family visit."

"I phoned the Buford house, asking for Della. Somebody named Odessa told me that Della had quit. Just like that. No two-week notice or anything."

"That *is* strange."

"Yeah. Another dead end. I'm beginning to run out of people to ask about the past, about my mother. You suppose the Smiths were also told to get out of Dodge?"

"Could be. Otis was part of the old crowd. I wonder what exactly happened back then," he mused.

"Something to do with my mother and the fire?" She sighed.

She sounded depressed. "When did you say you're seeing Dr. Harrison?"

"I was going to wait to see him when he comes back to Browne's Station, but now I think I'd better keep my appointment with him in Lexington."

"Wish I could go with you, but I'm on duty."

"I'm all right. Dr. Harrison isn't pushing for a fast breakthrough. We're going back slowly, so I shouldn't have a traumatic reaction. But thanks for offering." She smiled at him before she left.

Chapter Sixteen

Quentin's trip to Mt. Hebron had been a waste of
time.

"Well, maybe not a complete waste," he added when
he told Merrilee about the trip. Accepting a cup of tea,
he said, "I hope you don't mind my coming by this
late, but I wanted to make sure you got back okay. Did
you have a good trip?"

Merrilee shrugged. "The drive to Lexington was fine,
but the session with Dr. Harrison was a waste, like your
trip to Mt. Hebron. I didn't remember anything important. Just everyday kinds of things about Willadean and
a Sunday school picnic at Bridie's old country place."

She drank some tea. "What did Mr. Wallace have to
say?"

"The day of Brother Cosgrove's revival, Mr. Wallace was so sick, he couldn't even get out of bed to

look out the window to see who was coming and going. He was upset at having missed the excitement of the revival."

"That doesn't help us break Bridie's alibi."

"No, but when I showed him the photo of Bridie you found among your aunt's belongings, he thought it was Sula Jennings. At least until he noticed her clothes and hair. Apparently Sula always wore dresses, never slacks, and the church forbade women to cut their hair."

"Did he think the photo might be of Sula's daughter?"

Quentin nodded. "Mr. Wallace won't swear to it in a court of law, but he doesn't see how she couldn't be."

Excitement brightened Merrilee's face. "Remember what he said about Sula's daughter? That she might turn out to be an even better serpent handler than her mother?"

"Yes. The problem is that we don't yet have a single piece of evidence connecting her to any crime. No fingerprints—nothing."

Weariness replaced the excitement on Merrilee's face. "So Bridie might get away with murder. She took Aunt Hazel from me, and she won't even be punished."

Quentin reached for Merrilee's hand and squeezed it. "She won't get away with it. Plus, she has to buy her snake-handling equipment from somebody. She's got to keep her snakes nearby. You don't go out and find them just like that. All that leaves a trail."

"And the digitalis. Where did she get that from? Did she make it from foxglove flowers? Did she grow those herself?" She paused and frowned. "I don't even know what those flowers look like."

"A tall spike with bell-shaped blooms on it."

"I'm impressed," Merrilee said.

"I looked that up in the public library," Quentin admitted somewhat sheepishly. "I also have someone making discreet inquiries about what's growing in the Cosgroves' backyard. Sooner or later we'll get the answers to some of these questions, and that'll lead us to unravel the case."

"I hope so."

"It'll happen." Quentin saw exhaustion cloud her eyes. "You look beat. I'd better go and let you get some rest. I'll call you the minute I find out anything."

All morning Merrilee sat at the piano, determined to complete Hazel's song. She played the finished melody, hoping it would lead her to the refrain. Merrilee never knew from what part of her mind and soul the music sprang, only that this morning the source remained stubbornly uncooperative.

Perhaps she wouldn't be able to finish the song until the case was solved and Hazel's murder avenged. Hazel had been such a kind and gentle soul that she wouldn't even want revenge—but Merrilee did.

They needed physical evidence. Something to do with the snakes. Merrilee paced some more. The snakes had to be fed, so the wooden boxes or cages in which they were kept and transported had to be somewhere near Bridie but not in the parsonage. Too many people came to visit there.

Bridie's old place in the country? Under hypnosis Merrilee had remembered a Sunday school picnic there. Why? It hadn't been connected to the memory that preceded it. There was no reason for her to remember that meadow so vividly, unless . . .

The property was located in one of the hollows bordering Fox Creek. Did the Cosgroves still own it? Remembering the fierce pride in Bridie's face when she told Willadean that she had managed to put a down payment on the five acres, Merrilee was willing to bet her favorite guitar that they still owned it. She was also reasonably certain that she could find the place.

She stopped at the police station, but to her great disappointment, Quentin was out. Mace told her he expected the chief back shortly, but Merrilee was too keyed up to wait. She wrote a note, telling Quentin that she might know where Bridie kept her snakes. She added a simple map and directions to the place.

The second time she turned off Fox Creek Road, she found Bridie's old home. Even though in late autumn the meadow looked different, the small barn was still there, helping identify the place. The barn looked tidy with its fresh coat of red paint.

Merrilee hesitated. Then, reminding herself that the snakes wouldn't be slithering around free in the grass, she started toward the barn. With each step closer to the barn, her heart beat faster. She told herself that she would only steal a quick look through the small window. Snakes couldn't get at her through the glass windowpane.

Unfortunately, the view through the window was

blocked by boxes stacked up against it from the inside. Merrilee thought there might be a window on the barn's opposite wall. Rounding the corner, she found her path obstructed by bushes. Rather than going back around the other way and losing time and perhaps her courage, she worked her way through the thicket.

The moment Merrilee reached the other side of the barn, she stopped dead in her tracks. Although her eyes took in a car and cages with a woman bent over one of them, holding a stick, it took a second before her brain registered and accepted what she saw. Her heart seemed to stop when Bridie straightened up and faced her.

"You! How did you find this place after all these years?" When Merrilee remained silent, Bridie added, "Never mind. Actually, this works out perfectly. I can get rid of you once and for all. Dead, you won't be able to contest Hazel's will."

"So, it *was* you who killed her," Merrilee said, her throat and mouth so dry, she could hardly get the words out.

"I couldn't take a chance on her changing her will. I couldn't lose that money. Not after all those years of scrimping, of getting by, of making do. I'm sick to death of being poor and having to pretend that I don't mind because I'm married to a preacher."

"Knowing my aunt, she would have given you some of the money. She was kind and generous. You didn't have to kill her."

"Wrong. She was surprisingly stubborn and tough for such a scrawny old biddy. Had her mind set on giving the money to her only blood relative: you. So now I have to take care of you too. Ever been bitten by a copperhead? Hurts something fierce."

Merrilee couldn't keep herself from shuddering visibly.

Seeing Merrilee's reaction, Bridie elaborated with malicious glee. "Feels like being thrown into a fire. Since I haven't fed my beauties yet, they're mean and feisty."

"You won't get away with it!"

"Sure, I will. This will look like an accident. You went snooping around, tripped, and got snake-bit." With a triumphant look, Bridie continued. "I got away with giving Hazel the foxglove potion, didn't I? It was easy."

Merrilee bit her tongue to keep herself from telling Bridie that she wasn't going to get away with it. Casually she asked, "Where did you get the foxglove?"

"Grew them right here on this property. I have a small garden over yonder."

Merrilee glanced in the direction Bridie pointed. When she looked back, the serpent handler had snatched up a copperhead. Merrilee gasped. Then anger matched her fear and loathing. "You put that snake on my porch, and it was you who dropped your snake-handling stick. It was you who sent those notes."

"Yes! If you'd left town, everything would have been all right. But, no, you had to be stubborn." Holding the snake with both hands, Bridie said, "Let's get this over with."

Sweat broke out on Merrilee's face. Her body shook with terror.

Seeing Merrilee's face, Bridie smiled. "Good. Snakes can smell fear. Makes them even bolder."

It was the smile that galvanized Merrilee. Adrenaline shot into her bloodstream. She wasn't going to be Bridie's second victim. And she was going to make the woman pay for taking Hazel from her.

Careful not to look at the snake directly, she said, "Chief Quentin Garner knows I came here. He's on his way right now." From the frown on Bridie's face, she knew the snake handler hadn't counted on that.

"Won't do *you* much good," she growled, and she took a step forward.

After all the jogging she had done in her life, Merrilee was certain that she could outrun Bridie, if she could only get around her. The thicket prevented her from going back the way she had come. She would have to run the other way, between the wooden boxes with their slithering contents.

Merrilee repressed another shudder. The boxes had glass lids. Bridie wouldn't have been so careless as to leave the lids off and allow her snakes to escape. First she would have to do something to distract Bridie. Preparing herself for her move, Merrilee took a deep breath.

"Did you hear that?" she asked. Then she gazed over Bridie's shoulder with an expression of great relief. She even managed something like a smile.

Bridie turned to look. In that instant Merrilee

sprinted to the right, out of striking range. She *ran* as she had never run before. She heard a bellow of rage. In her peripheral vision she saw Bridie stumble and fall. She heard the splintering of glass, followed by screams. The screams pursued Merrilee in her headlong flight, filling her with terror, blinding her vision, spurring her on. All she wanted was to get away. She didn't stop until she ran into a solid body. Merrilee cried out and recoiled.

Strong hands gripped her shoulders. "It's me, Quentin. What's wrong? What happened?"

Her vision cleared. Seeing Quentin, she burst into tears. Between sobs as harsh as her breathing, she said, "Back there. Bridie. The snakes. She planned to kill me with a copperhead. She tripped and fell. I think her snakes got her." Shudders so deep shook Merrilee that Quentin had to hold her tightly to keep her upright.

"You're all right. Nobody is following you. Merrilee, I'm going to have to ask you to wait in my car. I have to see what happened to Bridie."

"No! The snakes." She clung to him.

"They won't get you. You'll be safe inside the squad car. I have to go. Do you understand?"

She nodded. "Go."

"I'll be back as soon as I can."

"Be careful."

"I will."

Merrilee sat in the car and hugged her arms around her waist. She rocked back and forth, unable to stop the small keening sounds that escaped between her bloodless lips.

After a while Merrilee heard a gunshot. What was happening? Did Quentin need help? Was he in trouble? Terrified to face what was behind the barn, but even more afraid that Quentin might get hurt if she didn't go, Merrilee opened the car door. She got out of the car. Just then she saw Quentin running toward her. He seemed unhurt. Merrilee sagged against the car to wait for him.

"What happened?"

"I've got to radio for an ambulance."

Merrilee listened to Quentin give their location, ask for a backup unit, an ambulance, and an antivenin kit.

"The victim's been struck repeatedly by at least one copperhead, maybe more. She's bleeding from cuts she sustained when she fell on a glass cage cover. I had to shoot a copperhead that was trapped between the victim and the broken glass. I saw the snake strike her twice before I could shoot it. The victim's alive but in bad shape. What can I—"

Merrilee covered her ears with her hands. She couldn't bear to hear any more. Her knees felt so weak, she allowed her body to slide down the side of the car. She hunkered down on the ground until Quentin touched her shoulder and helped her up.

"I want you to get back into the car and stay there."

"Where are you going?" she asked, alarmed.

"I'm going to stay with Mrs. Cosgrove until the ambulance gets here."

Merrilee nodded and scooted into the backseat. She watched Quentin remove a first-aid kit and blanket from the trunk of the car. She watched him until the barn hid him from view.

It seemed forever before she heard the sound of an approaching siren. A squad car, preceding the ambulance, pulled up next to Quentin's car. Bob Lee, a second officer, and two paramedics carrying a stretcher rushed toward the barn.

Again time dragged on and on. Finally they returned. She couldn't watch when they placed the stretcher into the ambulance. Bob Lee stayed back while the other officer drove the squad car, its siren clearing the way for the ambulance.

Quentin opened the car door. "We'll stay until the humane-society people get here. They'll decide what to do with the snakes that are still in the cages."

Merrilee nodded that she understood.

Quentin took off his leather jacket and handed it to Merrilee. "Put this on," he said gently. "It shouldn't be much longer before we can leave."

"Thanks."

The humane-society van arrived just before sunset. The driver loaded the cages into the van. After it drove off, Quentin returned to the car.

"Merrilee, give me your car keys. Bob Lee will drive your car to your house. I'm taking you home with me."

She didn't argue. Going home with Quentin sounded great.

They were silent on the way to his house. Charlie greeted them in his usual enthusiastic manner, but after petting the dog briefly, Quentin led Merrilee into the house.

"You're too pale. You need something hot and sweet

to drink," Quentin said. While the water in the teakettle came to a boil, Quentin built a fire in the fireplace. "Sit here," he said, pulling an armchair close to the flames.

He sweetened her tea liberally. When he noticed how her hands shook, he held the cup to her lips. He made her drink the entire cup quickly.

"What would you like for supper?" he asked, refilling her cup.

"I don't think I can eat."

"Yes, you can. How about some soup and toast? Or—"

The ringing of the phone interrupted him. His responses were terse and noncommittal, as if he didn't want Merrilee to know the details of the conversation. She sensed that it involved her. She got out of the chair and came to stand in front of him.

After hanging up, he said simply, "Bridie Cosgrove is dead."

"Oh, my God. I wanted her punished, but not like that. Not by being bitten to death by copperheads. She said it was like being tossed into a fire." Merrilee trembled. "I didn't mean—"

"Stop it," Quentin said, his voice gentle but firm. "It's not your fault. Your wishing her punished didn't cause her death. She did."

"All those snakes. How awful."

"Don't forget that she died the way she meant for you to die."

"Still, I should have stopped and tried to help her instead of running away."

"Don't talk nonsense. How could you have helped her? You don't know how to handle snakes. I had to shoot one to get to Bridie. No one in his right mind would expect you to stop and help a woman who seconds earlier tried to kill you. Her death is not your fault. You were the intended victim."

Merrilee didn't weep. Quentin wished she would. Anything was preferable to the trembling that shook her body. He touched her face. The skin was cold. He led her to his bed, where he wrapped a quilt around her and covered her with a comforter.

"Don't leave," she said. "Not until I fall asleep."

"I won't." He pulled up a chair and sat by the bed. He took her hand in his. If it reassured her, he would sit there all night long.

The next time she woke up, sunlight filtered through the blinds. Merrilee was in the bedroom alone. She remembered having a nightmare and then falling asleep again with Quentin holding her hand.

She sat up in bed. At the foot of the bed, on a navy robe, she saw a piece of notebook paper.

Curious, she scooted forward to read the note. It told her that Quentin had received an emergency call but that he would be back as soon as he could. In the meantime, she was welcome to whatever was in his fridge. He had already made a pot of coffee. She did as he suggested.

When he returned, Merrilee was sitting on his front porch, cradling a mug of coffee. The dog sat at her feet, looking at her adoringly. Quentin took off his sunglasses and sat down beside her.

Studying his face, she asked, "What happened?"

"The digitalis *was* in the sassafras and licorice tonic that Bridie gave your aunt."

Merrilee placed her mug on the floor and clasped her hands tightly in her lap. "So she killed Aunt Hazel because she might have changed her will. She killed her for lousy money."

"Money and love, or the flip side of love, are the most common motives," Quentin said. "Did you sleep okay?"

"Yes, thank you." She looked out over the valley.

Quentin watched her silently for a few minutes. Her thoughts seemed to be troubled. "What are you thinking?"

"Well, it seemed that Bridie's motive explained everything that's happened to me, but it doesn't."

That had occurred to Quentin as well, but he wanted to hear her take on it. "What doesn't it explain?"

"Ferlin Young. Bridie couldn't possibly have known him. She didn't even come to Browne's Station until after I'd lived with Willadean for a couple of years. And they certainly wouldn't have been in the same social circle."

"True. I couldn't find any connection between them."

"It seems to me that there are other people who want me to leave very badly. For instance, the Buford women. And whoever sent Ferlin Young to spy on me. Don't you agree?"

Quentin wished that he could disagree with her, but he couldn't.

Taking his silence for agreement, she continued. "Bridie Cosgrove had profit as a motive, but why do these other people want me gone? As far as I know, I have never done anything to any of them. I never even met the Bufords until a few weeks ago. It makes no sense to me. Does it to you?"

"No. Not yet."

"Except they all knew my mother. All except me. Isn't that supremely ironic?"

Seeing the quivering of her lips, Quentin took her hand in his. "Merrilee, don't. You'll drive yourself crazy."

"And Della and Otis Smith, who definitely know something, have disappeared."

"I've put an APB out on them. I want to ask them some questions," he said grimly. "We'll find them."

"Where do you suppose they went? And did they leave of their own free will?"

"That's hard to say, but I'd guess not. There's a strong connection between Otis Smith, Deke Buford, Ferlin Young, and the sheriff that goes way back," Quentin said.

"Something that also involves my mom and the fire. According to Pet Buford Mainwright, my mother also knew Earl Mainwright. I had the distinct impression that Pet was jealous of Reba. Maybe my mom and Earl were more than just co-workers in the bank. That would explain Pet and Lurlene's dislike of me."

"It would," he agreed. It would also explain the resemblance between Merrilee and Crystal that Naomi had mentioned. And the sheriff's interest in the case. Chapman had led the shoddy investigation into Reba Ingram's death. He probably knew, or at least strongly suspected, who had started the fire that killed her, and he had looked the other way. For a price? For re-election?

Chapter Seventeen

Merrilee had to speak to Della again. Taking a chance that the Smiths might be back, she drove to their trailer.

They weren't there. Discouraged, she stood by her car, looking at the deserted place. The sound of an engine made her turn around. The long, sleek Lincoln stopped beside her. Deke Buford got out of the car.

"Miss Ingram." He raised a hand to his hat.

"Mr. Buford." He wore a white, long-sleeved shirt, firmly buttoned, but no tie, which gave him an unfinished appearance.

"What are you doing here?" he asked.

"I was looking for Della Smith."

"What do you want with her?"

Merrilee didn't like his interrogative tone, but ingrained politeness made her answer him. "She knew my mother. I wanted her to tell me about her."

"I knew Reba too. Get into my car, and I'll tell you all I know, and I know plenty."

Merrilee could almost hear Willadean's voice warning her about getting into a car with a stranger. That was silly, of course. She was no longer a child. Still, there was something about Deke Buford that put her on guard.

"It's a lovely, sunny day. I'd rather be out here. So, you knew my mother?"

"Sure did. She worked in my daddy's bank."

Though it was not uncommon in the South to hear a grown man refer to his father as *Daddy,* Merrilee found it a little infantile. She waited for Deke to continue.

"To say that Reba was pretty is like saying that July sunshine is a little bit warm. And she knew she was a beautiful woman. She took full advantage of it. There wasn't a man who didn't respond to that smile of hers."

"Including you, Mr. Buford?"

"Sure. Why not? I was a young buck back then, full of energy and hormones."

"Did you date her?"

"I did plenty of fetching and carrying for her."

That wasn't exactly dating. Merrilee thought she detected a slight note of resentment in his voice. How badly had he resented being assigned the role of "fetching and carrying"?

"But I didn't mind. It was good to be around Reba. And then she got married."

"Did you know my father?"

"Just casually."

"Were you surprised when she married him?"

"Could have knocked me over with a feather. I didn't even know she was dating Rafe. She couldn't have known him long."

At least three months, if Merrilee's birth certificate was accurate, and she had no reason to think it wasn't. Then it hit her: Deke knew her father's nickname, which suggested that he knew him better than "just casually."

"And why on earth she married him, I'll never understand. He didn't have two nickels to rub together. At least not when they got married. He seemed to have come into some money later, but he ran through it pretty quick. No offense, Miss Ingram, but Rafe was not a great catch."

"He was a good musician, though," she added, feeling compelled to defend him.

Deke shrugged. "Didn't do much with it."

He obviously hadn't liked her father back then and still resented him. Had Deke been more than a little infatuated with her mother?

"She must have had a hard time, emotionally and financially, after he was killed," Merrilee said.

Deke shrugged. "I suppose so. She could have married again. Any number of men would have jumped at the opportunity, but she announced she wanted to leave town. Dumb move, if you ask me."

"Why a dumb move?"

"This was her home. Nowhere else could she have gotten the support she got here."

His vehement tone tempted Merrilee to shrink back, but she stopped herself. "But she never got a chance to leave, did she?"

"Get into the car, and I'll tell you more about her."

His tone, half wheedling, half threatening, caused Merrilee's hand to furtively search behind her for her car's door handle.

"I need to head back," she said. Just then Quentin's car pulled up beside hers. He got out.

"Hello," Quentin said, his eyes flicking between Merrilee and Deke Buford. He stood next to her, his gaze fixed on Deke. His stance indicated that he wasn't going to leave anytime soon.

Deke got the hint. With a barely civil good-bye, he got into his car and drove off.

"Am I glad to see you," Merrilee said, and she linked her arm through Quentin's.

"Was he coming on to you?"

"No. His attitude was more . . . threatening. He offered to tell me about my mother, but he kept trying to get me into his car. There's something odd about that man."

"With Lurlene Buford as his mother, does that surprise you? She uses that little-girl voice to wheedle, to threaten, and to dominate. She controls everyone in her family. Everyone except her son-in-law, Earl Mainwright."

"How on earth did a man like him end up marrying Petulia Buford?"

"That's the one impossible question to answer about any marriage."

"I suppose it is. Anyway, I'm glad you showed up. How did you know I was here?"

"My deputy saw you head this way. Looks like the Smiths aren't back. What are you planning to do next?"

"Go back to the courthouse. I need to look up something."

When she didn't explain, Quentin didn't press her for details. Merrilee would tell him when she was ready.

Merrilee looked up Dr. Edwards' phone number. He had been the medical examiner who handled her mother's case. When a female voice answered, identifying herself as Dr. Edwards, Merrilee was momentarily speechless.

"I was hoping to contact the Dr. Edwards who was the medical examiner here thirty years ago. Or his successor."

"I'm Irene Edwards, his daughter and his successor. What can I do for you?"

Merrilee explained that the records of her mother's death had disappeared. "Did your father keep personal records of his cases?"

"He didn't keep official records at home, but he kept detailed diaries."

Merrilee audibly caught her breath. "Do you have those diaries? And if so, could I look at them? Actually, I need to look at just one of them."

"You haven't told me why you need to look at the report or what my father might have written about your mother's death in his diaries."

"I'm beginning to suspect that my mother's death wasn't an accident."

"Have you talked to the authorities about this?"

"Yes. Chief Quentin Garner shares my suspicions."

"If you bring the police chief with you, you're welcome to look at the diaries."

"Fair enough. Where and when?" Merrilee carefully wrote down the address and instructions on how to find the doctor's house.

"Find anything yet?" Merrilee asked Quentin, turning the last page of the diary she'd been reading.

"No." Quentin took the next diary and handed it to Merrilee. Then he took one for himself.

Halfway through the diary, Merrilee sat up straight. "This may be what we're looking for. The date's right." She scooted closer to the lamp on the end table. She read the passage out loud.

"Did autopsy on Reba Jones Ingram, who died in a fire at her cabin. No doubt in my mind that she died from smoke inhalation, but there was a good-sized lump on the back of her head. From part of the roof collapsing? Most likely. And yet, it reminded me more of an injury caused by a blow to the head from behind."

Merrilee grabbed Quentin's arm in excitement before she turned the page. The next day's entry did not mention Reba, but two days later there was a brief notation.

Officially Reba Ingram's death is being attributed to the fire. Best for all. Best for her little girl.

Merrilee flipped through the rest of the diary, but there were no further references to her mother or herself. She turned back to the two pertinent entries and read them again.

"Sounds as if Dr. Edwards was protecting me."

"That's how I read it too. The question is, from what? Or, better, from whom?"

"The hands and the purple snake," Merrilee whispered and shuddered.

Quentin took her hand in his and squeezed it. Then he rose to look for young Dr. Edwards. Merrilee followed him. They thanked the doctor warmly and left.

At her house, Merrilee fixed a pot of tea, which they shared at the kitchen table.

"You think it's possible that someone hit my mother over the head to render her unconscious so she couldn't get out of the cabin?"

Quentin nodded. "Dr. Edwards suspected that as well, but something made him think you might be in danger if he voiced that opinion."

"But I don't remember what happened," Merrilee protested. "And everybody knew I couldn't remember. I couldn't even speak for several days."

"Whoever is involved in this was and probably still is afraid that you might remember."

"I was only four years old."

"It's possible, even likely, that you were a witness."

"If I didn't remember within a few days, what makes someone think I'll remember all these years later?"

"Possibly guilt. Certainly fear. There's no statute of limitation on murder."

"Oh, God. I never should have come back here." Merrilee cradled her head in her hands.

"You really believe you shouldn't have come back?"

Merrilee looked at Quentin and slowly shook her head. "Something made me come back. I guess deep down I need to know what happened. I just didn't expect to run into such violent emotions and old resentments. I still don't know what the Bufords hold against me."

"Deke Buford seems to have been in love with your mother. So he's a rejected suitor."

"And he still minds after all these years? And resents *me* for that? Isn't that a little crazy?"

Quentin shrugged. "As you said before, he is more than a little odd."

"Then there was that confrontation with Petulia Mainwright. She obviously hated my mother. And she said that really strange thing. Something about Earl's marrying her even though she wasn't as pretty as Reba."

Quentin raised an eyebrow. "Maybe Earl Mainwright liked Reba too. They worked together."

"But my mother chose Rafe, who, according to popular opinion, was a fiddle-footed musician without money and an aversion to matrimony." Merrilee didn't add that since her mother had been pregnant, he might have felt compelled to marry.

"How's the music coming?" Quentin asked.

"Changing the subject?"

Quentin grinned and glanced at his watch. "I'd better go and relieve my deputy. Do you have any food in the house?"

"Peggy brought some vegetable soup, and I have a noodle-and-beef casserole in my freezer. But that's big enough to feed two, so I'll save it for when you can stay for supper. If you want to stay sometime."

"I'd love to."

Merrilee walked Quentin to the door.

He stopped and gently tucked a strand of her hair behind her ear. Then he turned to go. "Regulations be damned," he murmured. He bent and kissed her thoroughly.

"Lock up after me," he said before he left.

Merrilee paced the length of her kitchen. Lately she seemed to do a lot of pacing, but it helped her think.

In their last phone conversation Quentin had told her that Della and Otis Smith had been found hiding out with relatives on an isolated farm. They claimed they knew nothing. At least nothing that they could swear to in a court of law. And, yes, Deke Buford had suggested that Della take a long vacation.

Merrilee was too impatient to stay put, but what could she do? Pausing at the kitchen table, she glanced at the *Evening Standard*. According to the lead article, Earl Mainwright was in town to give his election campaign a final push.

Staring at the article, she made a decision. Earl Mainwright had known her mother. Maybe had even liked her a lot. She had to speak to him. The article stated that he would be at his campaign headquarters. She called information for the number.

The man who answered the phone sounded vaguely familiar. He told her that the lieutenant governor was about to leave, but if she hurried, she could speak to him briefly. She should wait by his car, which was parked in back of the building. And she would have to come immediately.

Merrilee would have liked to change into something

a little dressier than her jeans, sweatshirt, and sneakers, but she couldn't take a chance on missing Mainwright. She drove rapidly to the election headquarters.

The old loading-dock area was empty except for Deke Buford's Lincoln. She parked next to it.

"If you came to hear Earl speak, you just missed him. He left for a meeting at the Businessmen's Club."

Merrilee slumped against her car.

"I'm going there. If you want, you can ride with me. I can get you a few minutes with Earl."

As much as she disliked Deke Buford, she knew this was her best chance, maybe her only chance, to talk to Earl Mainwright. "I'll follow you in my car."

"They won't let you in at the gate. Members only. You can come with me. Or not. Suit yourself."

Merrilee hesitated for a moment. Then she slid into the passenger seat beside Deke.

Wiley Chapman spotted the familiar Lincoln. As it passed him, he caught sight of the passenger.

"What the hell? That dumb, chicken hick is panicking again. He'll ruin everything and expect me to clean up after him. Well, not this time. I'm not covering for that mama's boy again. Miz Buford can find someone else."

The sheriff picked up his mike and called the dispatcher. "Get me Chief Garner."

"Just where is this Businessmen's Club?" Merrilee asked as they headed toward Laurel Mountain.

"Out in the woods. One of those modern cabins, all

stone and glass. Nothing like the real cabins that used to be out here. Like at Piney Creek Hollow."

The mention of the place where her mother's cabin had been caused Merrilee to look more closely at the landmarks they were passing. "Isn't this the way to Piney Creek Hollow?"

"Yup. What place more fitting to talk of the past than the spot where it happened?"

"You know what happened?" she asked.

"Sure do," Deke said with a smug smile.

Merrilee didn't like that smile, but then, she didn't like anything about Deke Buford. He had been Ferlin Young's friend. Had Deke . . . ? She had to ask. "Do you know what happened to Ferlin Young?"

"He got greedy. He was hired, to keep an eye on you, but he kept wanting more and more money. Like always. "He got into a fight over it. Things got out of hand." Deke shrugged. He glanced at Merrilee. "I was sure you'd guess the truth when I mistook you for my niece, Crystal."

"I'm told we have the same color hair. That's not so unusual."

"That's not all you have in common."

There was that annoying smirk again. "Why don't you just come out and tell me what you're getting at?"

"If we put you two next to each other, people would think you were sisters. That's because you are. Half sisters, anyway. Why do you think Pet sent Crystal off to schools far away?"

"Half sisters? Crystal and I?" Merrilee shook her head, bewildered. "Rafe Ingram is Crystal's father?"

"God, you're dense. Rafe's nobody's daddy. Leastwise, not that I know of. Reba got him to marry her when she found out she was pregnant with Earl Mainwright's baby and Earl was long gone. Mama's money must have made marriage to such a beautiful woman even more appealing to Rafe. Too bad he drank it all up and went and killed himself."

Merrilee's head spun. Earl Mainwright was her father?

"Earl didn't know about you. Still doesn't. And he won't find out if I can help it. Anyway, when Mama learned that Earl was hot for Reba, she made him an offer he couldn't refuse: lots of money and a job as assistant to a senator. Before he knew what was happening, Earl was on his way to Washington. A few days later he married my sister."

"I would have thought him a more principled man."

Deke shrugged. "He is, but as I said, he didn't know about you, and Mama can be mighty persuasive."

Merrilee's mind was reeling. She didn't notice where they were until Deke had turned off at Piney Creek Hollow. "Why are we going to the old place?"

Deke didn't say anything as he stopped the car. He took a handkerchief from his pocket and wiped sweat from his forehead. "It's a little hot in here." He took off his jacket and tossed it into the backseat. He wore a short-sleeved shirt under it.

Merrilee stared at his left arm, revulsion coursing through her. She was looking at a purple snake.

"Like my tattoo? Got drunk one Saturday night and woke up the next morning with this snake on my arm.

Mama pitched a queen-sized hissy fit." He raised the arm toward Merrilee, who shrank away as far as she could. With her hands behind her, she searched for the door handle.

"Put your hands where I can see them," Deke snapped.

When Merrilee glanced at him, she looked straight into the barrel of a wicked-looking handgun. She swallowed. "You're . . . you're going to shoot me?"

"Well, not here. I don't want to ruin my car."

"Why do you want kill me?"

"Because you were there that night. You saw everything."

"But I don't remember anything!"

"Not right now you don't. Maybe you won't tomorrow either. Maybe not even next month, but I can't take that chance. And I can't take the chance of your telling everyone that Earl is your daddy. Might ruin his political career."

"Why would I tell anyone? I don't need a father, and I gain nothing by ruining someone's career. And if Earl loved my mother and she him, I can respect that." Merrilee had to ask. "Did *you* kill my mother? What did she do to you?"

"I asked her again to marry me. She just laughed. Said she was going to Earl. She was going to tell him the truth. She was going to persuade him to leave Pet and run off with her and you. I couldn't let that happen. It would have disgraced my family. Broken Pet's heart. Shamed Mama. I had no choice."

"Is that what you've been telling yourself all these

years? Is that how you justified killing a young mother whose only crime was that she didn't want to marry you? And don't give me that garbage about protecting your family's good name!"

"Shut up! I thought the fire would be blamed for her death, and it was. Until you came back and stirred things up." Deke got out of the car.

Merrilee tried the door handle again, but it was locked. A moment later Deke opened the door. "Get out," he ordered. "I'll finish what I started all those years ago."

With a gun pointed at her, she had no choice. "Where are you taking me?"

"To a nice, deep ravine, where no one will find you. Or if they do, you'll only be a pile of bones. No more mistakes, like leaving Ferlin in the cemetery. Now move." He gestured with the gun.

Merrilee took a couple of steps, but, hearing the sound of a car, she stopped.

"What the—" Deke's voice was drowned out by a loudly shouted command to drop his gun.

Merrilee saw Sheriff Chapman, his pistol raised. Then everything happened at once. Shots were fired. Merrilee saw the sheriff clutch his shoulder and fall. In that instant she broke free from Deke's hold and dove into the thicket to her left.

Branches tore at her clothes, grabbed at her hair, cut her hands, but she fought her way through. On the other side was a narrow path.

She had run on this path before. She'd heard the crackle of flames, her mother's voice calling after her to run, then her mother's scream and silence. Then a man's footsteps, chasing her.

Merrilee ran uphill until she thought her heart would burst inside her chest.

She heard voices yelling. Heard shots that sounded different than the ones she'd heard earlier. Rifles?

The opening to the magic place, as her mother had called it, had to be in the rock formation up ahead. Somewhere in there was a narrow opening that led to a deep hollow with caves and other hiding places. If only she could find the opening in time.

She stopped, bent forward to catch her breath, and looked at the rocks. Years had passed. Trees had grown. The place didn't look the same.

She listened. She heard him thrashing on the other side of the thicket. It was only a matter of time before he would fight his way through. Instinctively she chose the middle rock to look at for the opening.

She heard a voice yelling for Deke to stop. He didn't. To drop his weapon. She doubted that he would. Then another shot rang out, and the thrashing stopped.

The silence that followed was like a long, suspended breath.

She heard her name called by the voice she knew and loved. Quentin.

She was safe.